Murder in the Neighborhood

Murder in the Neighborhood

JEFF O'DONNELL

Murder in the Neighborhood
Copyright © 2019 by Jeff O'Donnell. All rights reserved.

No part of this publication may be reproduced, stored in a retrieval system or transmitted in any way by any means, electronic, mechanical, photocopy, recording or otherwise without the prior permission of the author except as provided by USA copyright law.

This novel is a work of fiction. Names, descriptions, entities, and incidents included in the story are products of the author's imagination. Any resemblance to actual persons, events, and entities is entirely coincidental.

The opinions expressed by the author are not necessarily those of URLink Print and Media.

1603 Capitol Ave., Suite 310 Cheyenne, Wyoming USA 82001
1-888-980-6523 | admin@urlinkpublishing.com

URLink Print and Media is committed to excellence in the publishing industry.

Book design copyright © 2019 by URLink Print and Media. All rights reserved.

Published in the United States of America

ISBN 978-1-64367-595-4 (Paperback)
ISBN 978-1-64367-596-1 (Digital)

18.08.19

This book, my first, is dedicated to the special women that have been in my life and have changed it for the better. Lura (Belle) O'Donnell, Connie O'Donnell, Paula Davis, Lura Sanchez, Erin O'Donnell, and Quin Marceau. Each one has a special place in my heart yet alone in my life. Take just one away and I'm a completely different man.

I HAVE QUITE a story to share for those who like a murder mystery, a whodunit Thriller. The beauty of this story is I didn't have to go to the movies or get a book. No. It literally came to my front door. But first, let me introduce myself. My name is William- that's the name on the birth certificate, but as most Williams go, it turns into Bill. I'm forty-six years old and have a full head of hair that I keep very short on the sides but leave myself enough on the top so I can run my fingers through it when I get stressed out or when I'm trying to remember where I put something that I need right now. I tell everyone I'm six feet tall, but it's closer to five -feet eleven. I'm ten pounds over two hundred and should lose ten pounds to suit my body frame. But all in all, I'm feeling pretty good about myself. You see, I've been off work for more than six months and if the doctors are right, I'll be off for almost six more. My occupation before the injury was in construction. I was in cement work, mostly pouring foundations for commercial buildings, sometimes houses if work got slow. It was at one of those aforementioned jobs that I got hurt; it was kind of my fault and just some bad luck. I was trying to take a shortcut across the job site by jumping an open trench –the depth of the trench where I made my futile attempt to jump across was about nine or ten feet deep. As I took flight, I landed on the other side—clearly thinking I had made it with no problem, but my moment of triumph was short-lived; the bank gave way and I went crashing down awkwardly hitting the pipe below with damaging force to ankles and knees so that put me on workers' compensation where I am now.

I spend almost every day at home which is located on a very peaceful cul-de-sac containing about sixteen to eighteen homes – I say sixteen to eighteen because I never really paid attention. I've been here for a little over twenty years. And I could only name maybe three of my neighbors. Everybody does his or her own thing, if you know what I mean. Some are older couples that just stay inside and have someone come and cut their lawns and sweep up the front; you don't see much of them. Then there are the younger families. They drive up and down most of the day, taking or dropping off kids to school, and on weekends it's off to Little League or soccer – I don't know which unless I see what kind of uniform they're wearing that particular day. Then the last group on the street, they're the ones about my age: late forties, early fifties, you know the kind – the ones who still do their own yard work, wash their cars in the driveway, and still put up Christmas lights each year. They have teenage kids who play their music so loud it rattles the windows when they drive by but if I'm outside they always wave to me and make me feel I'm not a complete nerd. But enough already with the neighbors; what I want to do is bring us to this morning.

Today, the way it started, how there was no inclination or premonition this day would be so different. But I remember thinking to myself, *What a day!*

It's cold and damp and I'm not going anywhere, staying inside, have no reason to go out in this miserable weather. I'm still in my bathrobe standing over the coffee pot watching it slowly drip into the glass pot; it seems to be brewing at an agonizing pace. As I stand there rubbing my chin with its two-day growth, I'm thinking about what my mom told me many years ago: a watched pot never boils. I didn't care. I wasn't waiting any longer. I pulled the pot out, letting the coffee run all over the counter, and poured myself a cup. I got a dish rag, made a quick swipe across the steaming puddle and tossed the hot wet rag into the sink. I could hear a splash as the sink was half-full of dishes and dirty water. I thought *I'll get to that later today.*

Right now I'm going to sit down and drink my coffee and read yesterday's newspaper that's *still sitting on the end table where I set it yesterday*. No sooner had I flopped myself down and put the mug to my lips than the doorbell started to ring and ring nonstop; I'm thinking, *Wow! I know it's cold outside but give me a break. It's not a friggin' blizzard.* I yell out in a half scream, "Hold on, I'm comin'." As I start toward the front door, the ringing stops and pounding begins; as the pounding continues on my way to the door, I lose my cool and in a full yell say "Wait a minute!" As I reach the door, I grab the doorknob and swing it open very fast, more out of frustration than curiosity.

As the door is now wide open, I see a young man – mid to late thirties; clean shaven and well-groomed; hair was cut like you see police officers or military men; trying to hide under his arm was a very small and very young little girl. I'm not good at this type of thing, but I would say she was no more than seven or eight years old tops. I just look at the two of them, wondering what the hell their story is. I don't say a word; I just look at him then glancing back down at the kid, I'm trying to see if I'm missing something here. Finally, after what seems like several seconds, the guy says, "Can we please come in? Something terrible has happened." I am still silent; I just step to one side, keep the door wide open, and let them come into the house.

Before they got too far into the house, I moved quickly ahead of them to remove the dirty laundry that was piled on the couch. I grabbed the small stack and threw them into the chair I was just sitting on. I then reached over, got my coffee cup which was still warm to the touch, and held it as I ask the young man, "What's the matter? Do you need help?" As I looked at the young man, it seemed like I had seen him before; I was trying to think, *Where do I know this guy from?*

It was then he said, "You don't know me, but I live down the street from you –two houses down and on the left side of the street." I then pretended to say, "Oh yeah, I know. I've seen you outside before. I know who you are, what's wrong?"

He then held the little girl closer to his side and said, "We just came home from the bakery. We went up to get some freshly made pastry and bring it back for breakfast. We were only gone twenty or thirty minutes at the most. When we got home, I felt cold air coming from the rear of the house. I yelled out, 'Hey, babe, what's going on, do you have the back door open?' There was no answer from her. I thought she went out to the backyard for something real quick and left the door open, thank God I told Mags to hang up her coat." He then nodded down at the little girl. "Because she didn't get to see what I saw, I can't go into it now," he said, again looking down at what I presumed was his daughter. "I need you to call 911 for me, I think my wife has been – " Then he mouthed the word *murdered*.

"Please call the police, there – " Again he mouthed the words "might be a slight chance she's still alive, but what I saw" – he shook his head – "I don't think so."

I said "Sure," then I didn't know what to do with the coffee cup in my hand – take it to the sink, take a sip, set it right back down where I got it from. That's when I realized I was in shock; my mind was moving in ten directions at the same time. I thought of running out the door down the street to see if I could do something to help the young woman, run to the phone, call 911. Should I do something for the little girl huddled under her dad's arm? I took a deep breath and told myself, *Calm down, they came here for help, so let's help them.*

I then went to the kitchen, grabbed the phone, took it down my short hallway and into another room to make my call to the police; it was one ring when a female voice comes on the phone and asks, "What's your emergency?" I quickly answer, thinking if I don't respond fast enough she will hang up on me; I think I'm still in the shock mode. I say, "Yes, my neighbor just came running over telling me he thinks his wife has just been murdered." She then asks me what the location of this emergency. I then covered the mouthpiece of the phone and yell down the hallway, "What's your address?" He then yells back to me, "5226 Glenheaven Drive." I, in turn, repeat the address back to the dispatcher; she tells me she will have someone on the way immediately. I say thanks and then push the off button. I then return to the front room, finding them in the exact same position I left them. My mind was still darting from one thought to another; I thought, *why did he tell me the street name after he gave me the house number? Didn't he remember I lived on the same street? I knew it was Glenheaven Drive. I just needed the house number*, but that's what panic does to you – you just can't think straight. All your actions don't really make sense or go together. It was like me not knowing what to do with my coffee cup; even the smallest decisions become difficult.

Now that I was back into the presence of the dad and child, I asked them, either one of them, if I could get them something. I bent down and asked the little girl if she would like some hot chocolate; she sheepishly shook her head no, then while still bending down, I looked over at the young father and asked, "Is there anything I can offer you?" Like the little girl, he shook his head no but added, "Thanks so much for answering your door and taking us in." I said it's no problem; I'm glad I was home. That's when I thought, was there no one else home closer to his house? A next-door neighbor on either side, I was up the street and on the opposite side of his place, and he comes to me. Have we become a society where we won't even open our doors for a neighbor if it looks like they need help or, heaven forbid, in danger? Was I the only one who would open his door? Just then I could hear the sirens getting closer, so I put my hand on my neighbor's shoulder and said, "If you want, your daughter can stay here while you talk to the police." He looked up at me and said, "You know, I don't even know your name."

And for some unknown reason, I say, "That's OK, son, I don't know yours either. I never in my life called another man 'son', no matter his age, but it seemed like the right thing to say at the time. He told me his name was Roger; I then told him my name was Bill. He then asked again if it would be all right if he left his daughter with me. I told him there would be no problem; it would be better for the both of them if she stayed. He stood up and grabbed my hand with the two of his; it was then I noticed how much taller he was then me, and his double-handed grip was hurting me. I don't think he realized how hard he was squeezing; the adrenalin was pumping through his veins, and him being completely unaware of his added strength, he then released my hand and bent back down to look in his daughter's eyes and told her, "Maggie, please stay here with Bill while I go see if Mommy's all right." She then grabbed his arm with both of hers and pleaded, "Please don't go, stay here with me." Again she pleaded the same request before he could answer the first; he then told her in a very soft but comforting way, "Please, Mags. It's very important I go back home by myself. It could still be very dangerous, and I don't want anything to happen to you so please, for me, please stay with Bill. I won't be gone a long time, I promise."

With that, he removed the little girl's grip without too much of a struggle and headed for the door. I told him that Maggie would be fine and we would be right here when he came back, I was glad I got her name without asking for it from her; this way it would seem like we had known each other before the emergency that just transpired. As Roger swiftly but quietly vanished from the room, I then took notice of the severity of the situation. I have possibly a murdered neighbor two or three doors down the street that happened only a few minutes ago. Where is the potential maniac killer? Why am I standing here thinking about this stuff and not rushing over to the front door and locking it? I now have a little girl in my house that may be part of what was supposed to be a complete family killing. How did I know? I didn't, but I could feel myself starting to freak out; again, my mind was in the Indy 500–racing faster than my body could move.

I didn't want the child to see me in panic mode, so I did as her father did only moments ago; I told her in a really calm voice, "I better lock my door, don't want any strangers popping in." I thought, *What a stupid thing to say, that's what they were ten minutes ago*, so I swing around after locking and dead-bolting the door and ask again, "Hey how about that hot chocolate now? I was just going to fix some for myself, my coffee didn't taste that good this morning, you know," I told her. "I once won a contest for making the best hot chocolate. It was at the state fair. There was a whole bunch of people that entered that contest, but I won the blue ribbon. You know what the blue ribbon means, don't you?" She sat up from the couch, tucked her legs under her butt and said to me, "Well, I would have to be real stupid if I didn't say it meant you came in first place. You just told me you won a contest making hot chocolate." I said, "Yes, you're right. I guess I was thinking I was talking to some little kid who wasn't paying me any attention. Sorry I treated you like some dumb little kid. But anyway, do you want to try some of my award-winning hot chocolate or not?"

Now here's what gets me – she undoes her sitting-on-her-legs stance, stands straight up on the couch cushions, turns completely around, now facing me, puts her elbows on the back at the top of the couch, and says this: "I'll have some of your famous hot chocolate on one condition." She then gives me a two- or three-second pause for me to ask her, "What's the condition, my young miss," and she says this to me in quite the defying tone: "Show me the ribbon, and we got a deal."

She had me; there was no ribbon. I was just trying to get her mind off the immediate problem. I had to come clean. I tell her, "OK, OK, you got me, I never won a ribbon for anything, and if I ever did, I don't think it would ever be in hot chocolate. I just keep underestimating you. I haven't been around young kids in a long time, and I never knew kids your age were so smart, so what do you say we start all over again?" She looks me right in the face and says, "Just don't treat me like a child, and we will get along just fine." I tell her straight-out, "Miss, you've got a deal, so do you want something to drink, or can I fix you something to eat?" She then tells me, "Bill, I don't want anything to eat or drink, what I do want is to find out if my mom is all right." It's at this point I start to see the little girl that's been holding together so well start to crack. Her voice is shaky; her eyes well up with tears. I go over to her, I grab her shoulders, I drop to my knees and tell her, "You hang in there, your dad will be back soon, and he will let us both know, but it's OK if you want to cry. That's the one thing about sadness, it doesn't matter how old you are. If you need to cry, it's OK, there are no rules or age requirements. And listen to me, you got every reason to let loose." I had no sooner finished that last sentence than she put her arms around my neck and broke down and sobbed.

As I held the little girl, it felt like my arms could wrap around her twice; she was that small. I could feel her chest going in and out really quickly; I could hear her sobs down in her whole body. I felt so sorry for her, I mean a down-deep-to-my-feet sorry, but no words would come to me; and for some unknown reason, it seemed like the right thing to do, just be silent and let her sob as long as she needed. My inner self didn't try and analyze the situation; my inner self told me continue to hold her, don't say anything, and she, Maggie, would let me know when it was time to let her go. It didn't seem like it was a long time, where it started to feel awkward; it all played itself out in a minute or so. I could hear the sobbing let up, and her breathing started to slow down. It was then she slowly pulled away and wiped her eyes with the inside of her fingers. She was now standing a couple of feet away from me and saying, "I do this, right after I tell you not to treat me like a child." Her voice was firm and not a hint of quivering in it. I stand back up and look down on this small person and wonder to myself again, *Are all kids this age so tough?*

I tell her straight-out, "If this thing that just happened to your mom happened to me with my mother, they would have me in the back of an ambulance giving me some kind of sedative to calm me down, and that ain't no joke." Just then, there was a knock on the front door. I make a mad dash for the door. I open it up, hoping for good news about the mother. I see Roger standing there very solemnly and ask. "Is there any news of what happened?" He opens the door and comes back in, slowly closing the door behind him, using both hands to do so. He then starts toward us, almost tiptoeing across the front room carpet. He goes directly to his daughter and puts one arm around her shoulder and looks down at her and asks, "How are you doing, kid?" She then looks up at her dad and says, "You know I just had a good cry, and I don't feel as bad as when you left to check on Mom. I can see in your face things aren't good, are they dad?"

"Well, Mags, I have always told you the truth, haven't I? Never made up stories or sugarcoated things for you, have I? Well, I'm going to tell you straight-out. Your mom is on the way to the hospital, and the paramedics told me it doesn't look good for her to make it through the night. They told me she lost a lot of blood, and most just can't survive with that much blood loss. Maggie, do you understand the severity of the situation?"

She looks at her dad and says, "Yes, I understand Mom is most likely going to die tonight or maybe on the way to the hospital." Her father, never bending down or hugging her or any other matter of physical comfort, tells her, "Yes, you're exactly right on your assumptions." I'm thinking to myself, *Am I getting this right? The dad says to his daughter, 'Your mom is almost guaranteed to die, and get used to it already.'* I'm thinking, *What do I know? The kid seems well-adjusted, so let him parent any way he wants. As the saying goes, different strokes for — oh well, you know how it goes.*

I'm just dumbfounded as Roger takes Maggie's hand and heads toward the front door. Just before he reaches the door, he stops, turns around, and says, "Bill, did you want to come down to the hospital with us? I know you have been a great help to Mags and me. I just want you to know you're more than welcome to join us. I feel like you're part of the family or something, if you know what I mean, or am I just rambling along not making any kind of sense?" I start to tell him I understand what he's trying to say when Maggie breaks away and heads straight at me and looks me in the eye, saying, "Oh yes, please come with us to see if Mom can make it through the night. It would mean so much to me if you came, please come with us. It would be better if there was more people there, you know at the hospital, prayin' for her to get better, plus the doctors would try even harder to fix her if they saw there were lots of people there waitin' for her to get better, wouldn't they Dad"

As she looked back at her father, he said, "Maggie – " A pause from him and he says, "The doctors will try their hardest no matter how many people are in the waiting room, come on, we gotta get going." Maggie asked me one more time. "Please be there with us. I want you there with me, I mean with us," she said. I knew it meant a lot to her; she was almost begging me to come with her. I looked into those little girl's eyes, and how could I possibly turn her down? I said, "You guys take off and go, I'll be along in a few minutes. I promise you, I'll meet you at the hospital in a half hour or so." So Maggie turned, ran back to her dad, held her hand out to be gathered in by her dad's, and out the door they went. I thought, now standing alone in the middle of the room, *What in the world do they want me for? Just a short while ago, I was an unknown neighbor. Now they want me at their sides during a very tragic time in their lives. How strange is this life we live?* I said to myself, *Hey, if I say I'm going to be there, then by gosh, I'll be there, so let's get hoppin', shower, shave, clean clothes,* and I thought, *Let's bring a Bible. I have one, I just have to find it. I haven't used it since* – pause for thought – *since I can't remember.*

It only took me fifteen minutes, and I was looking for my car keys. My hair may have still been wet, but I kept thinking about that little kid and how much she wanted me there at the hospital with her. It meant a lot to me to have a kid that age wanting me by her side. I have never felt like the kind of man any kid of any age would request to have me by his or her side. It felt good to be wanted like that; I was quite flattered. I never had any kids of my own, so this kind of affection from a young child was all an unknown area or dimension to me. We're talking an uncharted sense of feeling or concern or, dare say it, love. This small child I met only minutes ago has grabbed my heart and is holding on tight before I knew it.

I was looking for a parking spot, the drive to the hospital seem to take no time at all due to the daydreaming about a little girl called Maggie. I found a spot and started sprinting to the emergency entrance. As I was now slowed to a jog, as I went no more than fifty yards from my car, I was thinking, *What do I say, what do I do? Do I put Maggie on my lap? Do I give her a hug when I see her? I don't know what the protocol is. I guess I'll let her show me what she wants me to do or say. I know for one thing she can see through my phony BS. I must remember this little child knows the score and how bad off her mother really is.* Just then, as I was thinking how this reunion is going to play itself out, I hear Maggie's voice yelling out my name as she runs down the hallway straight at me. I see the tears streaming down her face. I come to a stop, bend down on one knee, and open my arms to grab her and give her a comforting hug. As she gets to almost arm's length, she lets out an almost quiet sigh. "Bill, she's gone, she's really gone, she was dead when the ambulance got here. The doctors never even had a chance to save her." She put her little arms around my neck, dropped her head on my chest, and just whimpered – no sobs, no talking, just quiet little whimpers.

As I was kneeling down, just holding on to this frail small young girl, I couldn't help but think, *What type of person would put a child through this kind of agony?* I whispered into her ear, "Maggie, I need to talk to your father, could you show me where he is?" She stood up and held her hand out so I could take it and said, "I'll show you were he was when he was talking to the policeman. It's in a room down this way, come on. I'm sure he's still there answering questions."

We walked a short distance down the corridor until she opened a door that said Conference Room on the milky white glass; it centered the door just above the doorknob. She just walked in as she knew she had every right to. As we entered the room, I could see Roger sitting at a table with a steaming Styrofoam cup in front of him. He looked up as Maggie and I came into the room. The first thing he said was, "Mags, don't be going off without telling where you're going, do you understand me?" She answers, "Yes, sir, I should have told you. I saw Bill come in, and I ran to him to let him know where we were at. I was wrong. I won't do it again, I promise." Roger then looks at me standing right behind Maggie and says, "I see you made it just like you said, and you made it in good time. I wish I could say the same thing for my wife. She died on the way, or did Maggie already tell you?"

"Yes, she did, and I'm so sorry for you and Maggie. I never met your wife, but she must have been quite a woman, judging from how her daughter behaves. And I'm sure you're at your lowest right now, being only minutes since you got the news. I don't know what to say, I have no words that would fit a situation like this. Roger, I'm at a loss, I can just repeat myself over and over. I'm so sorry, is there anything I can do that would help you out in any way? You just name it and I'll do whatever it takes." Roger looks at me and says, "Bill, there is something you could do for me. It seems Maggie has taken quite a liking to you, and let's face it, I think I'll be several hours answering the police's questions. Bill, I tell you straight-out, I got no kin, I mean any relatives in the area, and I don't want Mags to be up all night when I answer whatever it is that they're going to ask me, so to get to the point, would you mind taking her home with you? I know it's asking a lot, but I trust you, and the main thing is Maggie does too."

"I have no problem with that." Looking down, I ask, "Mags, is that OK with you?" She quickly answers, "Yes, I don't want to be at the police station all night." She looks back at her dad and says (not asks), "You will come and get me when you're done, wont you?"

"Yes, I promise, as soon as they're done with me, I'll come and get you and you can sleep in your own bed. Maggie replies, "It's a deal."

As I lower my arm so Maggie has the choice to take hold of my hand or not, I turn to Roger and tell him, "It doesn't matter what time it is when you get over to my house, just ring the bell and I'll be there to let you in." He doesn't say anything; he just looks at me, gives me a small, fake smile, and waves his hand to the sky. I then turn and walk out the door. I feel Maggie's little hand trying to wiggle hers into mine. I open my hand wide, wait for hers to slide onto my palm, and close around hers gently but with enough firmness to let her know I was there to protect her. We walked slowly down the same hallway she had just run down to greet me only moments before. We both stared straight ahead, never saying a word; it was though we knew we were about to begin a long and sad journey.

It wasn't till we reached the parking lot when the first words were spoken, and they were the words of a small child, the kind that, well, put me at ease if you will. The words first spoken came out as a question, and it was Maggie saying, "You tell me which row your car is in, and I'll see if I can guess which one is yours." I don't know if she was trying to get my mind off the death of her mother or if she was doing it for herself; she was a sharp kid, and I was never again going to underestimate her. I told her, "OK, Detective Maggie it's in this row here," I said, pointing to the row we were now in front of. "Do you want any clues, two door, four door, anything?"

"No, I don't want any clues, that would take half the fun out of the challenge." I said, "OK, you're on your own, but I'll tell you one thing, you only get two guesses, and that's it. I'm not spending two or three hours for you to come up with a selection. She says, "Oh no, Bill, I'll make only one guess, and that's all."

"OK, it's a deal." So we were walking extra slow down the aisle of parked cars, and all of a sudden I'm thinking, *I'll bet she's waitin' for me to slow down a bit when I get close to my car.* I say to myself, *See, I'm not going to underestimate this little kid again. She's too damn sharp, and for some reason, I don't want her to guess the right car because she already has me talkin' to myself as it is.* Then I stop in my tracks and say, "Hey, wait a minute, how do I know you don't already know what kind of car I drive? After all, we do live on the same street you know." She looks up at me and says, "Bill, what kind of fun would that be if I already knew what you drove, tell me."

"Well, I don't know, maybe you would start me thinking you had special powers or something, I don't know, just to fool with my mind." Then she says, "Boy, you can make a simple guessing game into a – " She pauses. "I don't know what." I say, "I'm sorry, I just can't get over how smart you are for your age, in fact, how smart you are for any age." She then says to me, "I'll bet you one dollar I can guess what car is yours right from this spot, without taking another step." I say, "You're on." I then look back toward where we came from then glance toward the way we were walking. There was only seven or eight cars left in the row. I'm thinking, *If she can do it, knowing the last car in the row was mine, she did a good job, a job well worth one buck.* I say, "Kid, you got yourself a bet, tell me which car is mine."

"Sure, first let me hold your keys, I promise I won't look and see what make of car yours is." I hand the keys to her, she hits the panic button, the car starts honking its horn, flashing its lights, and she very calmly holds out her hand with the keys dangling from her fingers and says, "Your car is the one on the end."

I look at that little girl and can't help but feel she is one cute little person. I smile at her as I reach for my wallet to give her one dollar she beat me out of fair and square. I said, "Hey, that was pretty clever." She said, "Yeah, but it's kind of sneaky, so I only bet you a buck." I said, "Let's turn that alarm off and get something to eat." She said, "That would be good, but can we get something and take it back to your house?" I say, "Sure, what do you feel like eating?"

She says, "It really doesn't matter to me, you're the one paying for it, so you should be the one who gets to pick." I say, "Well, that's very thoughtful of you, but I might choose something you don't like."

"I'll tell you what we can do," she says, "let's get a pizza, and we can get it half of what you like and the other half what I like, how does that sound?" I say, "Kid, you came up with a perfect solution, let's do it." So we pull out of the parking lot, pull onto the main drag, and look for a pizza parlor. It didn't take long to spot one, only a block or so from the hospital, which makes complete sense. We pull right into their private parking lot, the lot that had a big neon arrow pointing to the driveway saying Pizza Parking. I pull into an empty stall and turn to Maggie and say, "OK, what's on your half?" She says, "My half will be easy, cheese only."

"No problem," I reply, "in fact, that will be the same as my half." So I turn to get out of the car, and she quickly replies, "Hey, Bill, would it be OK if I go in with you? I don't want to stay in the car by myself. I turn back so I could face her and say, "Hey, Mags, I wouldn't have it any other way, you bet you're coming in there with me. Come on, let's go." For the first time, I saw a smile on her face; it made me feel really good in one way but broke my heart in another. I got out of the car and headed for the back, toward the trunk, so I could meet her halfway and take hold of that warm little hand that I had already become very fond of doing. We took each other's hand and headed to the front door of what looked like a very busy pizza parlor. I held the door open for her as she let go of my hand and headed in. She only took a few steps ahead of me and then stopped and waited for me; it was as though she didn't want to be more than a couple of feet away from me. I could see she was so small, so alone, so very dependent on me. I felt so responsible for her emotions; it was as though I could break her with just one harsh word. I thought of the phrase "must handle with kid gloves." Boy, did that ever fit.

As I come the rest of the way in the door, I reattach my hand to hers and say, "Hey, kid, we better get in line or were gonna be here all night, just look at this crowd." She says, "Yeah, this place is always busy, my mom – " As she says the word *mom*, she drops her head and says, "My mom and dad like this place. I've been here lots with them." I say, "Hey, kid, it's gonna be tough on you for a long time. Don't worry about gettin' sad. Hey, I'm sad, and I never even met your mom." She then looks up at me and says, "You would have liked my mom. She was funny and she was smart." I said, "Then I know where you got it from. You must be just like your mom because I know you got two things your mom had, and that's a sense of humor and brains." She gave me a halfhearted attempt of a smile and says, "You know Bill, my stomach is startin' to make noises." I say, "It should, you probably haven't eaten all day, have you?" She says, "No. But I haven't been hungry before now."

As we move along in a line that was once eight to ten long, we found ourselves at the counter, and there we were met by a perky young high school-aged girl with a smile that fit her perfectly; her smile and words seemed very sincere when she asked, "And what can I get you guys tonight?" It was then I came to the fact that this young girl behind the counter or the people standing off to one side waiting for their orders to go or the ones that were already seated and eating and drinking, laughing, talking had no idea that this little girl, the one holding my hand and standing next to me, had just lost her mother in a brutal slaying. No, none of them had a clue; it was just as the saying goes, "Life goes on," but it should add to that, "Life goes on, with or without you."

The voice of the perky order taker snaps me out of my daydream and asks again, "Have you decided yet?" I say, "Oh yes, we want a large cheese pizza, and that's with extra cheese please." I look down at Maggie and ask, "Is that OK with you, the extra cheese part?" She looks up at me and says, "Bill, that's perfect, I couldn't have ordered it any better myself." I said, "You do know I know sarcasm when I hear it, don't you?" She said, "Yes, I was just teasing you."

"Well OK, let's stand over here with the others who are waiting for their orders to go." So we slid over a few feet to the small group that was waiting the same as we were. Behind the small gathering of waiting customers, there was a small couch, no one sitting on it, so I give a small tug on the hand I was holding of Mags, a motion with a gesture of my eyes, and a nod of my head toward the small couch, and she lets loose of my hand and scoots beneath the standing group and sits down quickly then pats the open space next to her for me to sit, but I couldn't scoot through as she did; I had to rely on the group to part their ways and give me an opening to squeeze through. They opened a path and never even looked at me; they moved away and separated as if they were in a trance, as they if were programmed to move when anyone gets too near body contact.

As I sat there next to Maggie, I didn't know what to say. I know I'm eventually going to ask her what she feels, what she thought happened, if she has any thought of who might have done this terrible thing. I thought I'll wait till she eats something, see if she falls asleep, see if she brings it up; in other words, I'll just wait and see how it plays itself out. It wasn't but what I thought were a couple of minutes and they called our number. The sweet perky one behind the counter looks over through what was now a new group waiting for their number to be called and says, "We've called your number, your pizza is ready." I thought to myself, *I never heard her call; I must really have my mind miles away from where I am now.*

I look over to Maggie and say, "Let's get the heck outta here." So I robotically make my way over to the section of the counter that has a sign above saying Pick-up Only, repeat the number that was ringing in my head, and say, "Thirty-six, number thirty-six, the plain cheese." This time I'm talking to a man with a well-trimmed beard, who says, "Would you like any beverages to go with that, sir?" I kind of have a feeling he is the owner or a manager of some type. Knowing the real mark-up is in the sodas or bottled water, I tell him, "Hold on, let me ask my partner if she wants something to drink with that pizza." So I glance down at her and say, "Well, what about it, kid, you want something to drink?" She says, "Don't you have anything at your house we can drink?" I think to myself, *she's pretty nice; she doesn't want to run the tab too high.* I tell her "No, not really, nothing I think you would like." She then says, "OK, I'll have a small root beer, that's what I always got when Mom and Dad took me here."

This time she got it all out, the mom and dad part, without dropping her head or having her voice fade. I repeated the order of one small root beer, and that was it; I knew I had some cold beer in the fridge, and that's what I always had with pizza, hot or cold. I took the large tan-colored box, slid my hand underneath, took the small container of root beer with my other hand, and gave it to Mags and said, "Let's get this puppy" – nodding my head at the box – "home before it gets cold." She headed in front of me to open one-half of the swinging glass doors; she – like a good doorman, held the door open, using her back and rear end to keep it open to its maximum width. I nodded and said, "Thank you, ma'am." As I stepped through the door, she was right behind me before the door was completely closed all the way. We made our way to the car and back to my house without any distractions of any type; the ride was very quiet, except for an occasional "I've been in that store" or some other passing comment that would remind me Maggie was indeed a very young little girl. As we got into the house, I had to turn on the lights. The long day had turned into evening, and my morning coffee seemed like a lifetime ago; and thinking of my choice of words, it was, a lifetime ago –a lifetime for Maggie's mom, which I now realized, didn't even know her name. I said, "Hey, Mags, let me show you where I keep the plates." She replies, "If it's all right with you, we just use paper towels at our house, or I should say 'we use to.' I don't think there are going to be any more pizza nights at our place, at least real soon, that is." I say, "Come on, Maggie, don't think like that right now. We got each other, and the pizza still hot, so let's enjoy it together, what do you say?" She looks at me and says, "Bill, you're absolutely right, plus my stomach says 'Come on, Maggie, put something in me.'" So I like the idea of paper towels and rip off a half dozen or so from the roll and head toward the kitchen table.

 I sat down at the table, gently sliding the box from the palm of my hand onto the flat surface; there were four chairs surrounding this very generic-looking kitchen table, with only one place mat and a pair of salt and pepper shakers standing on the mat, which was strategically placed in the middle. Maggie comes into the kitchen, still holding on to the cup of root beer, and proceeds to pull out a chair one handed. I tell her, "It might be a bit easier if you set that cup down then pull the chair using two hands." She doesn't answer me on my suggestion, she just does it, and at the same time she's pulling out the chair, she's looking at the place mat and says, "You don't entertain much, do you?" I say in a simple reply, "No, no, I don't. That's why it's such a pleasure to have you here with me. I eat alone almost every night." I go on to tell her, "Sometimes some of the guys I work with come over, and we might watch a ball game or something, and we will get something to eat or I'll barbecue something but that doesn't happen too often. Most of the time, it's just me, and that's OK. I kinda like it like that, if you know what I mean?"

She says, "Yeah, I kinda know what you mean but didn't you ever have a wife or any kids? You look like a guy that would have kids." I ask her, "What does that mean? I look like someone who would have kids? Explain what kind of look that is." She tells me as she's reaching into the pizza box, "Well, Bill, I shouldn't have said 'look like someone who would have kids,' I should have said 'acted as though they had kids,' you know what I mean? You can talk to kids, you can kinda understand what their thinkin', it seems to me, the way you treat me, you musta had kids a long time ago. You seem to know what to do or what to say, but you're just outta practice or something. You're thinkin' kids are dumb or somethin', it's like your outta touch, do you know what I mean?"

I tell her, "Yeah, I know what your sayin'." This time I'm the one reaching into the box to get me a slice. As I carry on with the discussion, I tell her, "No. I never had any kids and no, I never had a wife but I did have a girlfriend for a long time." She then asks, "Well, what happened to her, where is she now?" I say as I chew the pizza and continue to talk, not realizing how hungry I was, "Well kid, it's kind of a long story." She says, "I'm not going anywhere for a while, so let's hear it."

I ask again, "Are you sure you want to hear this? If you ask me, it's pretty boring." She says, "Yeah, I do." Reaching for another slice, I say, "OK, but before I start, do you want me to put the rest of that root beer in another glass with more ice?" She says, "No, it's just fine the way it is. Now get on with the story, you're stallin' around." I tell her, "No, it's not that, it's just something I don't think you'd be interested in." She says, "I'll never know until I hear it, will I?" I say OK, now thinking I lost my taste for the beer I was going to have, and for some reason, I wanted some of her root beer. I say, "Maggie, let me have some of your root beer, and I'll get started on that story." She looks at me and says, "Are you serious? Do you want some of my root beer, or are you still stallin' around?"

"No," I say, "I really do want some, just a small glass, that's all, honest." She says, "Go get a glass and I'll share what I have, it's more then I can drink anyway." So I stand up, push my chair back, and go get myself a small glass from the cabinet, come straight back, sit back down, pull my chair in, I think this is my opening, you know I never did ask you your moms name and slide my glass out across the table as to make it just a casual question no drama or build up just a passing question toward my dinner mate and say, "Just half in that and that's plenty." She removes the straw from the tightly fitted lid, removes the top, and fills my glass halfway just as instructed. She says, my moms name is Audrey, or should I say her name was Audrey as she pours her rootbeer I say, "Whoa, her name will always be Audrey. She then says as she turns the cup to its upright position, " yeah I guess your right, her name will always be Audrey, "Now that we took care of that, I would appreciate you continue with your story"

"Sure," I say. "Sure, her name was Lura, not Laura but Lura. We went to high school together, she was a year behind me. I met her when I was a sophomore and she was an incoming freshman. I remember the first time I saw her, she had a stack of books in her arms and was slowly walking down the hallway, trying to check out the numbers on the lockers. I thought, 'Wow, this girl is more than cute, she's a knockout.' You do know what knockout means?" I ask. She says, "Yes, I know what knockout means, see, that's what I mean about you thinking kids my age are stupid, and we're not, go on, what happened next?"

"Well, I saw this as my chance to meet her. I say, 'Hey, what number you lookin' for?' She glances down around the stack of books at a small slip of paper and says, 'Two one nine, its locker number two one nine.' I say, 'You're almost there, here, let me take some of those books from you, and I'll show you right where it is.' She says, 'No, I'll hold on to the books, you just head toward the locker and I'll follow you.' Yeah, that's how we met. After I showed her her locker location, I introduced myself and told her I would see her around, and I made sure I did too. I talked to her at lunch; I made sure I was always walking home the same direction she was even though I lived the opposite way; I made sure I was the one who asked her to the first school dance of the year. To make a long story short, we dated all through high school. Then after she graduated and a year or so went by, we moved in together. That lasted almost eight years, then things just started to change. She talked about marriage, kids, a place of our own, and the thought of a wife, kids, a mortgage, it seemed so final –like my good days would be over." That's as far as I got; she stopped me at it and says, "Bill, I need to lie down, I'll listen to the rest on your couch, if that's all right with you." I say, "No problem, kid. You have had one exhausting day. Come on, I'll get you a blanket, and we can continue this boring story of mine over there on the couch. I'll put this pizza away later, let's get you ready for the night. No telling how long your dad's going to be."

Maggie knows she's starting to fade, and she's very agreeable to the switch from kitchen chair to cushy couch. I walk directly behind her, thinking she may collapse mid-journey. I may not know too much about small kids, but I do know exhaustion when I see it and my new little pal was out on her feet. I throw the pillow that I'm holding to the end of the couch, hoping that will direct her to the waiting resting spot. Like a fish chasing a lure, she followed the pillow to her ready-made resting place. When she hit the pillow, she surprised me again; I thought for sure she would be asleep within seconds of head meeting pillow, but no, she says, "OK, Bill, you and Lura – not Laura, move in together, then what happens?" I say, "Are you kidding me, you still want me to continue?" A quick reply is an emphatic yes.

"OK, I'll continue on one condition, and that's you listen with your eyes closed." My little buddy says, "That will be no problem, I was going to close them anyway." So I have to ask her, "Where was I?"

"You and Lura had moved in together."

"Oh yeah." I start up again. "We found a place we both liked, moved in, and everything was going good. I had found a good-paying job in construction, Lura also got a good job with the school district as a girls' PE teacher. We were both happy with the way things were going. I was making so much money I bought a tiger for a pet." I gave a good pause after that tiger line and heard nothing. I looked down at the little sleeping beauty, and she was gone, and it made me feel good to see her look so peaceful; heaven knows she needed the rest, and hopefully, she could get five or six hours of sound, solid sleep.

As I was watching the little thing sleep, I slowly got out of the chair I had slid next to the couch and moved away at a cat burglar's pace. I went back to the kitchen to put the pizza away, taking one more slice before cramming it into the fridge. As I was rearranging the few items I did have in there, when I saw the beer, I now wanted it. I grabbed a can, turned, and closed the door as I always do, with the side of my foot. Went back to the kitchen table, pulled one of the chairs back out, and sat myself back down. As I opened the cold beer and hoisted to my lips, it was then I started to think, *Who kills a young housewife?* If she was a housewife, I didn't even know that. Housewife or not, I did know she was a mother of a young child, and someone murdered her; my question was not so much who but why? As I was contemplating my question, the phone rings. I jump like a jack-in-the-box to grab it before it wakes Mags. I get it on the first ring and almost whisper into the receiver, "Hello." On the other end is a voice I don't recognize; it says, "Bill, is this Bill?" I say, "Yes, who is this?" The answer came back, "It's Roger, Maggie's father." I say yes. Before I can tell him his daughter just went to sleep, he says, "Hey, I gotta ask you a big favor, can she stay with you till morning? I got a feeling the police are going to be questioning me all night. I say, "Sure, it's probably best we don't wake her anyway." He is quick to say, "Yeah, you're right. I'll call you when I'm headed your way." I start to ask him a question when I hear the sound of click; he hung up the phone. I think this seems very strange to me.

Roger hangs up the phone not even asking how his daughter is doing. I think that would be the main reason for the call in the first place. I'm starting to have a different opinion of this Roger character. I look over at the couch and check to see that Maggie hasn't woken up. Luckily, she hasn't. I start to pace the room, not knowing what to do next. For some reason, I felt the urge to go look at the neighbors' house and see for myself what happened there; this whole murder thing is just what Roger has told me. True, there were police and ambulances down the street, but I never saw anybody being loaded up into any ambulance, don't remember the police asking me if I saw anything. I was at the hospital; it was there the police could have asked my name, how I know Roger and Maggie, and all other pertinent questions the police usually ask, but no, they just serve hot coffee at the hospital and concentrate on only one person, the husband. I've seen enough crime T.V. programs that it's almost always the husband, so I guess they – the police, will be headed my way in due time.

As I continue pacing throughout the house, contemplating all the possible scenarios, I just can't get over this feeling, like the house down the street was a magnet just pulling me, a force stronger than my mere body or mind could resist. As I kept up my uncontrolled pacing, I thought, *I could sneak down there for a minute or so*. Maggie would be out for hours; she was warm, safe, and I would lock the door. It wasn't as though I was going out to a movie or something; I was just going down the street, just a couple of doors down. Right, listen to me, trying to convince myself it would be OK to walk out on this kid, sleeping or not. Here I was only moments ago criticizing the kid's dad for not asking about her, and I'm ready to walk out on her; now who's the real dick between the two of us? I tell myself, *I'll wait till she wakes up, and then I will work out some sort of plan to get a look at that house before it's swarming with media, police, and every curious onlooker within the city limits.* I didn't have to wait long; Maggie sits up, throwing the blanket off to one side, and says, "Did the phone just ring, or was I dreaming?" I tell her, "No, you weren't dreaming, your dad called to check in on you and also told me he was going to be longer then he thought." She then grabs the blanket and puts it across her lap because she now is sitting straight up.

"You know," she says, "Dad's been a lot different since this [she pauses], I don't know what to call it. Since this situation, tragedy, killing, I guess the best thing to call it is a nightmare." I'm quick to respond with, "Yes, that's the best word I think you could use, nightmare, that sure describes it." But I go on when I ask her, "What do you mean your dad's been different?"

"Well," she says, "my dad's not one who usually asks how I'm doing, where I'm going, or what I like, things like that, you know what I mean?" She goes on by telling me about at the hospital, how she ran to greet me and he tells her, "Hey, tell me where you're going."

"He never cared before when I would run around, and when we used to go for pizza like I told you about, he would ask me every time, 'What kind do you like?' And for him to phone and ask how I was doing, it's like he's a whole different Dad."

"Well, you got to understand he is going to be a different dad. He always let your mom watch over you and keep an eye on what you were doing. He put her in charge of all that stuff. Now he's going have to start doing all the things she did, and it's all going to be new to him."

"Well, I guess," she says, "but for him to phone and ask about me, that's pretty sweet of him with all that he has on his mind."

I smile and say, "You're right, but I think no matter what's going on with all the questions and stuff, I'm sure your number one on his mind. But now I have a question for you, I'm going to be straightforward with you, that's the only way I know how. Here is what I want to do, and you tell me what you think. My plan is to go down the street to your house and look inside to see if I can make any kind of sense of what happened yesterday morning. But I don't want you to go, I want you to stay here." She says to me, "I will stay here, but will you tell me if you find or see something that will help me understand what happened to my mom?" I tell her, "I promise, if I see anything that will help you feel better about you losing your mother, I will tell you everything." She lets the blanket fall to the floor and walks directly to me and reaches for me on tiptoe feet and outreached arms to hug me around my neck and tells me, "Bill, you're going to help me get through this sad time, aren't you?"

"Yes, I'll do whatever I can to make things better for you, but it's going to take a long time, you're going to be sad for a long time. The only thing we can hope for is that your sadness will start to go away with time, that's all we can hope for. Each day will get better and better. No matter how old you may get, you will always have some sadness that never leaves you, do you kind of understand what I'm telling you?"

"Bill, I understand, I'm going to be sad the rest of my life, just not as bad as I feel right now."

"Yes, that's it, you understand. I should have known that you're one sharp kid."

"What is your plan?" she asks me.

"Well, I plan on taking a flashlight and try and find a way in. If I can't get in, I will look through the windows. You wait here, your dad may come at any time." So with those simple rules, I got my flashlight and was headed out the door, only to turn right back in the house and use one choice word in front of Mags, *shit*. As soon as it came out of my mouth, I apologized. "Oh, I'm sorry, I hardly ever swear." She wants to know then what brought me to this moment of weakness that made me use such a descriptive word. I'm quick to respond, almost using another, "There's a cop sitting in his car, watching over the place. I don't know what I was thinking, of course they would be watching the house. It's a major crime scene."

Maggie says, "Bill, close the door behind you, come back in here, and we will make a plan." I tell her, "I don't know how the heck I can even get close to your house, with that cop out front. He's just sitting, doing nothing but keeping everyone away." There is now silence in the room; I can see in Maggie's facial expression she really wants to help. I'm back to pacing back and forth, rubbing my hair as I do when I'm stressing out on making what I consider big-time decisions. As nothing comes to mind, I'm thinking to myself, *I should just stay out of this*. It was then, just as I was giving up on any chance of me taking a look at the crime scene, I hear Mags break the silence. "Bill, I got an idea, you tell me if you think it will work. You take me down to the policeman in the car, you ask him if he can get one of my dolls for me, tell him I need it, I sleep with it. After you get his attention, then I'll start talking to him, begging for my doll, that's when you can check out if there is a way you can sneak around the side of the house. Once you make it to the side, it will be easy to get around to the back, that's where mom was when she got attacked. Our kitchen faces the backyard, plus there are lots of windows and glass sliding doors. I'm sure if you get back there, you will be able to see the whole kitchen."

"You know that just might work, if I see how your property is laid out, I will know if I can sneak around to the back without being seen."

We talked it over. I made sure she wanted to go through with trying to deceive the officer of the law, and she had no problems with our joint devised plan. So with no further words, I opened the door, and we made a direct path to our target, a patrol car. As we approached the car, the officer was already starting to roll down his window in full anticipation of an upcoming question. As we got next to the vehicle, the officer spoke first. He looks at me then at Maggie and says, "Isn't it a little late to have your daughter up?" I say, "Oh no, Officer, I'm just watching her while her father is being asked questions concerning her mother's death."

"Oh, I'm so sorry," he says as he looks right at Maggie. "What can I do for you? You know I can't let you in the house." She says, "Oh yes, I know I – or we – can't go in, but I was wondering if you could." As he starts to ask why, you could see the bewilderment in his eyes for such a puzzling request. As he started to explain why he was unable to go inside, Maggie, on cue, starts to explain the importance of her favorite doll, the one she can't go to sleep without.

As the officer tries to explain his unenviable position, I walk toward the back of his cruiser, looking at all angles of the property, trying to see the best way to sneak past the watchful eyes of Officer Watchdog. As I scan the area, I can hear Maggie start to plead, "Please, I need her, I have always slept with her." That's my warning to get back to the car where the officer can see me and not let him get any idea I'm casing the area. As I walk up alongside the driver's side of the car, I find that the officer has gotten out of his car and he's almost in tears that he can't do anything to ease a small child's suffering. I come to his rescue as I say, "Maggie, he can't go inside the house. If he did, he could lose his job." It's a quick response by the officer. "Yes, he's right, I would get in big trouble if I set one foot in that house, I'm so sorry, but I hope you understand." Maggie looks at him and says, "Yes, I understand, and I don't want you to get in any trouble."

He says, "Thanks, I'm glad you understand." It's at that moment I say, "Come on," as I put my hand out for her to grab, "let's get you back inside." The officer said, "It's too late for you to still be up." She gives me her hand and says, loud enough for the cop to hear, "I'm going to have to get used to be without lots of stuff." As we interlock hands, we head back to my place.

As we reach my front door, Maggie turns to me; she is facing me and at the same time searching for the doorknob with one arm behind her and saying, "You know, Bill, I think that went rather well." Before I can give her an answer, she's pushing the door open with her rear end. That's when I say, "Yes, you did a great job distracting him, and it was just long enough for me to see it's almost impossible to be seen once you're along the side of the house, because on the right side of your house there are lots of shrubs and overhanging branches from your neighbors' trees. The only thing I'm worried about is the flashlight. If I shine it into the kitchen, will he be able to see it from the front of the house?"

"No, I don't think so," she says. I'm quick to ask, "How do you know?"

"Well, it's the windows in the front of the house, they're up pretty high. If you shined your light low, I don't think he could see it." I look at her and just shake my head in amazement. She says, "It's just what I think. I don't really know what it's going to look like from the sidewalk out front."

"Well, you convinced me it's worth a try. Here's my plan, you and I are going to get in my car, we're going to drive down the street, we're going to stop at Officer Watchdog's car and roll down our window and tell him were going to the store for some ginger ale, you've gotta a stomachache, and we'll be back shortly. I just hope he doesn't ask us to bring him back anything." Maggie says, "It sounds like a plan to me, let's go." I say, "Wait a minute, I want you to put on my bathrobe, showing him you were trying to sleep when the upset stomach hit." So I look through the pile of clothes on the chair, find the robe with absolutely no hesitation, open it up for Maggie to be draped in, and go find my car keys then head out. We were on a mission, and we both were trying to find out some answers to what seemed like a senseless act of violence.

It only took moments, and we had found ourselves side by side with the stationary police patrol car. As I was now on the wrong side of the road, my driver's side was paralleled with the officer's. I rolled down my window as if I were going to place an order at a drive-through window. The first words out of the young officer's mouth was, "You know that's illegal, you being on the wrong side of the street, plus its dangerous."

"Yeah, I know, I'm just going to the store, the little one's got an upset stomach, so I thought some ginger ale might help."

"OK" was the answer back, then, as I was about to pull away, I hear, "Hey, maybe you could pick me up – " Then a pause and, "Oh, never mind, I was going to say 'pick me up a cup a coffee,' but that's not such a good idea, it'll just make me need to go pee." I say, "We will be back in a little while," taking off before he could change his mind about the coffee. It was only a few hundred feet before we were at the entrance of the cul-de-sac. It was then we made a quick left turn, and we were completely out of sight. I pulled the car over, making sure I didn't park directly in front of anyone's house. I cut the engine and turned to face Maggie straight on. I ask, "Are you going to be OK by yourself?" There is no hesitation. "Yes," she says, "go see if you can find out anything." I say OK; I then check my flashlight again, thinking it might have gone bad in the half-block jaunt. As I see it's still working fine, I tell Maggie, "It should only be five or six minutes, and I will be back to report my findings." It's then I tell her, "Stay low." I open the car door, trying to slide out without the dome light coming on; then find myself slipping into the darkness, but not before I make sure I lock the door and close it slowly and gently enough to only hear a slight click.

In the blink of an eye, I was crouched down and heading to my preplanned destination – Maggie's backyard, and looking into the kitchen, where I presume it was once a happy and wondrous place where the photos on the Bisquick box became a real-life culinary delight. But those are just memories of what I think took place in a house full of love; I had not the slightest insight of what I was about to witness through those glass windows and doors. In what was only seconds, I found myself crawling underneath low-hanging tree branches from Maggie's neighbors on the right. I was now on my hands and knees, making very slow progress along the side of the house. I knew the cop could see nothing from his vantage point. As the bushes and tree limbs started to thin out, I thought I might be able to stand up a little; my knee joints were screaming for relief. As I stood up, not quite fully, I took one more step, and *pow*, I hit my forehead on a wall-mounted air-conditioner; it sent me staggering back. I instinctively put my hand to the injured area, only to see blood on my hand when I checked for the results. I thought how careless I was, but I continued with no further delay.

I approached the end of the house and peeked around the corner, not knowing what I might see or find; luckily, it was clear. I went back down to the more uncomfortable crouch position and headed for the sliding glass doors. I'm sure the police left everything the way they found it; that meant no closed drapes or closed curtains, had a clear view of the crime scene. As I inched directly in front of the sliding-glass patio doors, I could see one kitchen chair lying on its side. Just a few feet in front of the chair, there was an overturned ironing board. By the board were a few items of clothing or towels; it was difficult to make out for sure. I was going to have to use my flashlight. I was still somewhat apprehensive to use my flashlight, but as Maggie had said, there were no windows in direct line to the front of the house. I switched on light, making sure I had it facing toward the ground. I then slowly aimed the stream of light to the kitchen floor area. It was then I saw smeared blood; it looked like two definite, separate smears, starting from down the chair, out toward the sliding doors, but the massive amount of blood was located between the fallen chair and the overturned ironing board. I did see what looked like a bloodstained hand print on the wall that was next to one or two bath towels that were lying on the floor. As I took one more glance, I could see most of the folded items undisturbed on the kitchen table; the thing I noticed most was the lack of damage, no broken glass or blood smears on the walls. Except for that one print, nothing on the sliding glass doors trying to escape, only a chair and ironing board overturned and folded clothes still untouched. It looked like an attack she never saw coming or one that she never suspected of happening.

As my mind ponders what could have taken place, it just seems so out of place, an unprovoked attack on a housewife in her own home. I take a quick glance at my wristwatch and know it's time to get back to the car. I don't want Maggie to start to worry. So I make my way back without any setbacks. As I open the car door, Maggie stays low in the backseat but wastes no time in asking, "Did you see anything that might be important?" As I get into the car, making sure the dome light is only on for a second, I tell Maggie, "I'll tell you what I saw when we get back to the house." She agrees. "Yes, let's get back." We drive down to the end of the street and then make a U-turn and head back to the house. As we make the turn onto our street, I make sure we don't slow to wave or even make eye contact; I didn't want to take any chance he would call us over for any reason whatsoever.

So things went smoothly; we pulled into my driveway and were about to get out when I told Maggie, "Hey, kid, you'll see a baseball cap there on the back seat. Bring it with you when you walk to the front door and carry it by the bill."

"Why do you want me to do that?"

"Because from a distance, it will look like you're carrying a bag, maybe a bag of ginger ale."

"Oh yeah, good thinking, Bill." As we get into the house, I look again at what time it is. I can't believe it; it's almost 2:00 a.m. I say, "Hey, kid, I don't know about you, but I gotta get some sleep." She had no complaints with my plan. She knew it wasn't a suggestion; it was a fact. I was going to get some sleep. She said, "I know where my bed is," pointing to the couch. I said, "I'm taking the recliner." We both headed to our selected spots, and we were both sawing logs in just a matter of minutes. As I was in a deep sleep, I was suddenly startled out of my slumber by the sound of my doorbell ringing. I have no idea how many times it had been going off, but I looked over to the couch and saw that the little one was still sound asleep. I jumped up and tried to answer the door before another ring went off. As I reached the door, I opened it.

As I stand there holding the door open, still half-asleep, I'm thinking, *It's Roger standing there.* I just assumed he was here to pick up his daughter, but my slumber is broken by the sound of a female voice asking, "May I come in?" I now look at whom I'm holding the door for. I reply with a staccato, "Oh yes." It's a somewhat attractive fortyish brunette, dressed in what looked like a tailor-made jacket with matching pants. As she enters the house, I explain, "I thought I would see Roger when I opened the door," and she, without hesitation, asks, "And who might that be?" as I take a better look at who I just let in my house, I see a police badge being displayed for my view. Then the words, hello I am homicide detective Quin O'Hara, may I come in? I say, "Yes, come on in," Then the detective suggests we head into the kitchen. I say, "Yes, please sit, and I'll start up some coffee." As I go to the sink to get some water to start the coffee process, she pulls out a chair the same time she's pulling out a small notepad from the inside of her jacket. No sooner had her derriere hit the wood of the chair than she fired out her first question. "The Roger you speak of, would that be Roger Hanson?" As I pour the water into the maker, I say, "You know, I never did ask his last name. It was all a whirlwind of an introduction."

"How's that?" she asks.

"I thought you knew all about this situation I'm in?"

"Why would I know that?" she said, giving me a squint of the eyes and a puzzling look.

"That's because your department has been questioning him for about twenty-four hours straight. And I would think after that many hours, you would know the whole story about his daughter and why she's here sleeping on my couch."

"Well, I'm very sorry, but I was just brought on board this morning, I have not had a chance to meet with the detectives doing the first interviews. Let's start again," she suggests. "As you now know, I'm Detective O'Hara, and you are?" I wipe my hands with a nearby dish towel and offer my hand and say, "I'm Bill Mathews."

She, in, turn extends hers; as we shake hands, I pull a chair out and sit down across from her. "So tell me, Mr. Mathews,

how did you come to the point of babysitting the daughter of a neighbor that you didn't even know the name of?"

I say, "Detective O'Hara, if you can't wait to get all the notes from your fellow buddies, I guess I'll tell you how it all came about." I then proceeded to tell her what took place from the point of them knocking on the door till we came home from the hospital with pizza. I never mentioned the visit to the crime scene. After I gave her what I thought was enough of the important information that she needed, this whole recap I gave her took me about twenty or thirty minutes. It was after I finished when I said, "Now can I ask you a question?" She said, "I don't know if I will be able to answer it, considering this is an open investigation." I say "No, this doesn't have to do with the crime, it has to do with your questioning Maggie's father, Mr. Hanson." She says, "What about him?"

"I would like to know how you can question him for almost twenty-four hours straight without charging him with the crime. Or have I missed something? Is he in custody?" She again gives me that puzzled look. "I don't know what your talkin' about. As far as I know, he was released a short time after he was told his wife passed away. But let me make a call and verify that information." She pulls out a cell phone and hits one number and is connected almost immediately. I hear the one side of the conversation; she says, "Yeah, that's what I thought, what time do you think that was? OK, thanks," then she flips the phone closed. She looks at me and says he was released to go at around 5:00 p.m. *Oh great*, I think to myself, *this asshole has been playing me.* She then asks me, "Why would you think he's been answering questions all this time?" I then put my finger to my lips and point to the couch.

"So you're telling me you've been with this kid since this whole thing took place?"

"Yes, and don't get me wrong. I rather she be with me than with her father, if that's what you want to call him. I like having her around, she's smart, and she's as sweet a kid as I ever met."

"Well, I'm glad you two are hitting it off because she's going to be needing support for a very long time to come. Also, may I ask you if you saw anything yesterday morning? Such as a car. You didn't recognize someone walking up or down the street that seemed out of place? In other words, anything out of the ordinary? Maybe you heard something?"

"No," I replied, "I didn't see or hear anything until the two of them came pounding on my door."

"And what time was that?"

"Oh, I don't know for sure, but I'd say around nine or a few minutes one way or the other."

"And tell me again what he told you."

"He said he and Maggie" – I then cocked my head in the direction of the sleeping one – "that they just went up to the bakery and got something for breakfast, they came back, he told me they were gone maybe twenty minutes or so, and found the house cold from the backdoor being left open. He then told me he called out for her, walked back toward the location of the cold air, and found her in what he described as a horrifying bloody mess. He ran back to grab his daughter, who was hanging up her coat, and swept her out of the house and brought her here to call 911. He did say he didn't think there was much of a chance she was still alive. He then asked if Maggie could stay with me. It was a short time after that when we could hear the sirens, and he left to go back to his house."

"OK," she says, "let me double check what you're telling me. Mr. Hanson comes to you, someone he doesn't even know, bypassing three other houses, drops off his daughter, asks you to make the 911 call, then stays, talking with you, and doesn't head back to the house to see if he can help save his wife's life until he hears the sirens close by, is that about how it took place?"

"Yes, as near as I can remember, but I was thinking the same thing, about why he came all the way up here, to my house. I was thinking maybe I wasn't his first choice, maybe the first house he went to, nobody answered, and not wanting that to happen again, and losing time, he saw my car in the driveway and went for the sure thing, meaning someone would be home to answer the door and let him in."

"That may very well be," she says, "and you know, that will be one of my questions for him, plus where he has been since he was released from questioning, and why has he not picked up his daughter from a neighbor he didn't even know just a few hours ago."

The conversation then switched from father to daughter. "I'm sorry, Mr. Mathews, but I'm going to need to ask Maggie some questions. I do hate to wake her up, but it's necessary I do ask these questions before too much time passes and memories start to fade."

I tell her I understand, but down deep, I really think it can wait till she wakes up, but I go over to her and bend down and begin to give her little shoulders the slightest of shakes. She slowly opens her eyes; she's still very groggy but manages to say, "My dad's here, isn't he?"

"No, I'm sorry, but I'm sure he'll be here anytime now, but there is a very nice police officer here to see you and ask you some questions. Do you feel up to some questions?"

"Yeah, I guess." She then attempts to sit up; as she's trying to sit up and cover herself, Detective O'Hara glides in and, with the tenderness of voices, introduces herself. "Hi, Maggie, I'm Detective Quin O'Hara, and I want you to call me Quin. First, I want to apologize for asking Bill to wake you but you must understand, I need to ask you some questions before you forget what you saw yesterday morning."

"I'll do the best I can," she says in a very low voice. Quin says, "Maggie, that's all I want," at the same time patting her on her knee.

Quin then starts by asking, "What bakery did you and your dad go to?"

"The one that's next to the hardware store."

"You mean the Ace Hardware store?"

"Yes," she answers back.

"Tell me, were there a lot of people in the bakery when you got there?"

"No, not at all, in fact, the only other person in the store was getting her change and was leaving the store."

"So tell me, did you know what you wanted, or did you look around for a while?"

"No, I knew what I wanted. I always get the same thing every time we go there. I get two glazed doughnuts and Dad almost always gets an apple turnover."

"What about your mom? What did you get for her?"

"Oh, she gets different stuff each time we go but most of the time she gets a blueberry bagel."

"And what about this time?"

"This time I remember my mom telling my dad, 'Why don't you guys surprise me?'"

"So did you guys try and surprise her?"

"No, we both were afraid we'd choose something she wouldn't like, so we both decided on the same old thing, a blueberry bagel."

"So did you drive right back home, or maybe you stopped somewhere else, maybe for juice, gas for the car? Anything?"

"No," Maggie says, very sure of the answers she has given.

"Well, you're doing very good. I only have a few more questions and I'm done." Quin continues, "What about when you got home? Did you both walk into the house together? Or did your dad go ahead of you?"

"No, we got out of the car at the same time, and we walked into the house together. It was after we got into the house we went different ways."

"What do you mean you went different ways?"

"Well, Dad went straight into the kitchen and was asking my mom, 'Do you have the backdoor open? It's freezing in here.' That's all I remember because after I hung my coat up, I was headed into the kitchen when my dad came running back and took my hand and said, 'We gotta get out of here and call 911. Something terrible has happened!' I tried to ask him what happened, and he said, 'I don't know, we just need to get help, and as fast as we can.'"

"So tell me, what did you and your dad do when you left the house?"

"We went next door, but nobody answered, Dad even pounded on the door with his fist. The door shook, but no one came, then I remember Dad saying a bad word and saying, 'Let's go up the street, there is a car in the driveway,' so that's when we went to Bill's house, and Dad was right, someone was home."

"And that's all you can remember about yesterday morning?" asks Detective Quin.

"Yes, that's all I can think of."

"You did great, Maggie, you really helped me out, thanks so much."

"You're welcome" was Maggie's reply. Just then, the doorbell rings; Maggie jumps up and heads for the door. Before the bell rings a second time, Maggie swings the door open, and this time it is Roger. Before he has a chance to say a word, Maggie's got her arms in the tackling position around his legs. "Whoa, let me get in the house there, kid." Maggie unwraps her arms and reaches up with one hand, almost begging for him to take it, but he doesn't instead he pats her on the head and walks into the house. "Hello" was the first word out of Detective O'Hara's mouth as she made a beeline to shake his hand and say, "Let me introduce myself, I'm Homicide Detective O'Hara." With her introduction I couldn't help but notice two things – she left off her first name while introducing herself, and I noticed Roger was quite refreshed, clean shaven, and wearing a fresh shirt. But I wasn't going to say a word; I thought, *I'll watch Quin in action*. I could always add my two cents at a later time.

Detective O'Hara got right to the questioning. I somehow feel better referring to her as Quin or Detective than that formal sounding O'Hara, but maybe that's just me. Anyway, back to Roger and his story about where the heck he has been for the past twelve hours or however long it's been since he was released to go about his merry way. One thing I knew for sure, I knew where he wasn't.

"So tell me, Mr. Hanson, would you like to make arrangements for someone to watch Maggie?"

"Why is that? I just got here and I plan to take her with me. I would like to spend time with her and maybe try and explain what happened, the best way a father can to a young daughter."

"Oh, that's so thoughtful of you, Mr. Hanson."

Roger snaps back, "It sounds like a heavy dose of sarcasm, Detective."

"Well, if the shoe fits, Mr. Hanson – "

"Detective, let's cut to the chase. What is your problem? You seem to have an obvious dislike for me."

"Oh no, Mr. Hanson, I'll have to ask you some questions and listen to your answers before I make a decision on whether I like or dislike you. And that's just what I want to do, I would like to meet you down at the station and ask you some questions. The first is where have you been since you were released to go and that was over sixteen hours ago?"

"OK, OK, I see where this is headed," Roger says as he nods his head up and down. "I will take Mags over to her grandmother's, then I will call my lawyer and meet you at your department in a couple of hours. Does that meet with your satisfaction, Detective?"

"Yes. That will be fine." After Quin and Roger's verbal exchange, Quin then goes over to Maggie and offers her hand. Maggie stabs her arm out palm open and smiles. As the two are shaking hands, I notice Quin takes her other hand and wraps it over Maggie's and says, "Thank you so much for your help. I want you to know how nice it was to meet you and I will do my very best to get the person who did this to your mother." As she left the side of Mags, Quin was headed in my direction, also hand extended for what I presumed would be a farewell handshake. "Good-bye, Mr. Mathews,

please take my card, and don't hesitate to call me if you think of anything that would benefit my investigation."

"Yes, you have my promise." As Detective Quin was heading out, Roger was instructing Maggie to get what she needed. "We're going to Gram's house."

Maggie then asked her dad a question – I was curious to hear the answer. She asked, "Did you tell Grandma what happened? Does she know Mommy's dead?"

"Yes, I called her from the hospital. I told her that she was attacked in the house but we don't know who or why someone would do that to her. But Grammy's first question was about you, she asked right away, 'What about Maggie? How is she doing? Please bring her to me, I want her with me.' And that's just what I plan to do. First, I'm going to take you shopping, I want you to pick out new pajamas, bathrobe, school clothes, and whatever you think you might need. And then when you get to Grandma's, you two can go out and see if there are other things you might need. So before we leave, I want you to thank Bill for taking care of you this last twenty-four hours." With that request from her father, Mags darts directly to me, and I bend down because I want more than a handshake; I want to give a hug and get one in return. Maggie puts her little arms around my neck and whispers in my ear, "I need to know what you saw in the kitchen." I whisper back, "I promise I'll tell you what I saw." I stand up and ask Roger, "If it's all right with you, I would like to take Maggie to lunch, maybe in the next couple of days or so?"

"Yeah, I think that will be OK," Roger asks Maggie, "Would you like that?"

"Yes, yes, I would like that very much" is her instant answer.

"Well, I'll tell Grams about Bill and explain that he might be coming to get you in the next few days." Roger then says to me, "Bill, I want you to know my mother-in-law lives just outside of town, it's about a forty-five-minute drive from here."

I say, "That's no problem. Just give me the directions and the phone number and I will phone and we can agree on a good day and we can go out for lunch." Roger then asks for some paper so he can give me the requested information. After writing everything down, he said, "I am very indebted to you, thank you so much for your help and understanding." With that, he shook my hand and was headed out the door. Detective Quin was still standing off to one side, waiting for Roger's departure, I was thinking, I bet she has more questions for me and sure enough as soon as Maggie and Roger were out the door she asked me just one question, she wanted to know if I saw any blood on Roger's body, shoes or clothing. I told her no, can't say that I did. And that was that.

She says thank you again, and tells me as she did with Mag's that I have been very helpful, then turns and walks out without another word.

After I close the door behind her, I was again alone in my house. It seemed very quiet and even kind of lonely without my little partner, Maggie. I was now thinking, *Just how do I explain what I saw when the time came to be with her? I know she's smart, I can't sugarcoat it too much, but I will just have to be a little less graphic when I describe what I saw,* but as I was thinking about my next visit with Mags, I couldn't help but have the vision of that kitchen in my mind – the sliding glass door not broken, the handle and lock not damaged. That meant the door was unlocked, or if it was locked, she opened it for whoever came in. Also, no bloody hand prints on door, neither inside nor outside. I think she knew her attacker; they came right in. Or she saw who it was and let them in. She – Audrey (finally asking Maggie her mother's first name), then turned her back to the attacker, never expecting the murderer would harm her. The way I look at the scene, Audrey was grabbed from behind, probably by the neck in a choke hold, then, my guess, she was repeatedly stabbed in the chest and heart area. She must have flung her arms and legs for as long as she could. I believe she was not only surprised but overpowered. I need to get the police report and the autopsy findings. When I get that, I would be able to compare my hunches with facts. Also, I don't believe robbery was the motive – unless they ran out of time when they heard the husband and child coming into the house. Whoever did this, ran out without closing the door or ,as far as I know, taking anything. But what kind of stuff would you kill someone for? Was this just a random burglary that went bad? I don't think so. My prediction is whoever went into that house was there for one reason –to kill little Maggie's mother and heaven forbid the possibility he or she will be back to kill the rest of the family. Maybe there was much more to this killing I could even imagine?

My thoughts of the murder made me very sad and very tired. My mind and body were telling me I needed more sleep – more than the three or four hours I got in my easy chair. So, I jumped in the shower then into my own bed; it felt so good, I was sound asleep in seconds. I woke up on my own, no doorbells ringing, no pounding of the door; I just woke up. When my eyes opened, I felt great, full of energy and ready to do what I could to help Maggie find answers and justice for her mother's brutal murder. I knew better than to get in the police's way, but I might be able to work with Detective O'Hara. She seemed like she would take help if it brought her closer to finding out the person or persons that committed this crime.

I thought, *What the hell, I'll give Quin a call and let her hear my thoughts on what I thought might have happened, but I don't think I will mention my sneaking into the backyard to look at the crime scene with my own eyes.* So I hunt down the business card Quin gave me and I give her a call. I get an answering machine, telling me she is away from her desk or she is out in the field, and try her cell phone number. So I scan the business card again and look for her cell number; there it was, so I gave that number a try, and after only one ring, I hear, "Detective O'Hara's." I say, "This is Bill Mathews on this end, and I would like to know if I could speak with you." She, very businesslike, says, "And may I ask concerning what?" I can't help but think to myself, *What do you think? The weather? Come on, you're a detective, take an educated guess.* But being somewhat of a gentleman, I don't give any of those sarcastic answers; I just say, "The Glenhaven place murder."

"Well, Mr. Mathews, it so happens that's right where I am now."

"Well, that will work out just fine. Would it be OK if I just walk down the street and talk with you?"

"No, I don't want you near the crime area, it's all taped off, and it's quite hectic. I will walk up to your place, and we can talk there."

I say, "That'll be fine," so I hang up and head outside to meet her at my walkway, the one leading up to my front door. When I get out there, I can see her talking with another plainclothes detective. I see her pointing up toward my direction then starts walking. I wave at her, but she just keeps walking, not acknowledging my friendly gesture.

As Quin reaches me, she then offers me a "How are you doing, Mr. Mathews?"

I say, "I'm doing fine, but I would prefer being called Bill."

"OK, then Bill it is, why did you want to talk with me? Do you have information concerning the case?"

"No, but I do have some theories I would like to share with you."

"Yes, I'm open to any thoughts you might have, but before you give me your thoughts, may I ask what happened to your forehead? I noticed it last night, but with Mr. Hanson walking in, I forgot to ask."

"Oh." As I put my hand over the wounded area, I say, "Gee." My mind goes blank; I forgot all about the collision with the air-conditioner, so as my mind is racing to come up with a decent answer, I know anything I say now will sound like a lie, so I just take my chances and tell her the truth. "Well, to tell you the truth, I hit my head on the air-condition unit down at Maggie's place. I went down there the other night to take a look for myself."

Quin snaps back, "Are you out of your mind? Do you know that you compromised the whole crime area? So the blood sample we got off the AC will come up as yours?" I put my head down and sheepishly nod yes. Quin then starts to say "Bill" but changes her mind mid-sentence and says, "Mr. Mathews, I will need to see you in my office this afternoon, until then, good day." As she turned to walk away, I was speechless.

The more I thought about what I did, the more I knew I screwed up. I had to go down to the police station and take my medicine. I could be charged with obstruction of justice or maybe become a prime suspect; after all, my blood is at the crime scene, and I have no alibi for the time frame that the crime was committed. I was downright worried as I was driving to the police department. When I got there, I had no trouble getting a parking spot; there was a section that had a sign saying Police Interview Parking Only. I got out of my car and headed to the four-story building. Actually, feeling physically sick, I kept going and found myself in the lobby, looking at the directory for Homicide Detective Quin O'Hara's floor and room number. There it was, second floor, room 212. I made a few steps to my right and pushed the button for the elevator. I was alone in the lobby, and I also felt very alone in my mood. The door opened as soon as I touched the button. I stepped in; it was empty. I hit button for floor number 2 and was off. The sudden lift didn't help my tender stomach in the least.

When I reached the second Floor, I could see a door to my right, it was room 212; written on the door below the number was the word that made my stomach feel very queasy, Homicide. I knew I was being expected, so I just turned the knob and walked right in. It was a much larger office then I expected. There was a desk in front of me as soon as I entered the room; at that desk was a uniformed female officer, I would say in her mid to late fifties. She looked very military, but when she smiled, she seem like a sweet and reassuring grandmother type. She put me at ease when she said, "May I help you, young man?"

I smiled back, trying to let her know how easy she made me feel. I said, "Yes, I'm here to see Detective O'Hara."

"Oh, she's down this way," and with that, she stood up and said, "I'll take you to her desk." So I followed the somewhat portly officer down several rows of desks, some with people at them, others silently empty, but I noticed all desks, vacant or not, were covered with paperwork. "I was wondering. Are there that many murders in this city that it takes that many full-time detectives to cover them all?" The next thing I hear is, "Please take a seat, Detective O'Hara will be right with you." I turn to see the nice uniformed officer holding the back of a chair, implying that's the chair I was to sit in. She then says, pointing directly to a glass-enclosed office, "She's talking to her boss." I sit and glance at the paperwork she has stacked in front of her swivel chair. I don't see anything with my name on it, like a warrant for my arrest. My spying is interrupted by the words, "Finding anything interesting, Mr. Mathews?"

"No, I didn't, but I have to admit I was wondering if there was a warrant for me, charging me for the murder of Mrs. – "

It was then Detective O'Hara said, "It's Hanson, her name was Audrey. She was thirty-two years old, but I know almost all I need to on Mrs. Hanson, it's you I need to know more about. That's why I had you come down to my office Mr. Mathews"

"OK, Detective Quin, ask me anything, I'm an open book."

"Very well, let me start with, do you have any objections with us, meaning the Riverside Police Department, searching your home?"

"None whatsoever, when would you like to start?"

"Oh, I think when you leave here, we will meet you at your home, is that OK with you, Mr. Mathews?"

And I say without any pause, "I will be waiting outside for you."

"That'll be great, but before we go do that, Is there any way you can prove you were home at the time the slaying took place.

"No, as I told you before, I was just about ready to drink my morning coffee when Maggie and her dad came to the door."

"Tell me, Mr. Mathews, did you just step out of the shower when they came to the door?"

"No, I didn't, you can ask them if my hair was wet."

"Oh, we will, I can assure you that."

"Wait a minute, just hold on, are you implying I took a shower to wash away any blood evidence?"

"Mr. Mathews, I never implied anything, you're the one who is doing the suggesting."

"That's it, I don't want to say any more without a lawyer."

"That's fine, Mr. Mathews, if you think you need one, I completely understand."

"No, no, I don't need a lawyer, I have nothing to hide, I'm just starting to stress out. I'm scared. I screwed up big-time going into the backyard, and I put myself in a spot where I'm a suspect."

"Actually, Mr. Mathews, you are the only suspect at the present time. You see, Mr. Hanson was with his daughter during the time frame the murder was committed. Now mind you, we're not saying Mr. Hanson didn't have anything to do with this, we are just saying he was not the one who did the actual slaying."

"How can you say that? Did you ask him why he didn't try and give his wife CPR or call 911 from his own house."

"Yes we did and his answers were consistent with the evidence we have."

"Well please tell me why he ran right out of the house when he found his wife lying on the floor bleeding to death."

"He said he was terrified the killer was still in the house and felt he and his daughter were in immediate danger, so he got out of the house as quickly as possible."

"OK, then let me ask you a couple of questions. Maybe my buddy Roger didn't do the actual killing, but did he have someone do it for him? I know you have been doing this type of work for a few years, and I'm sure that has to enter your mind."

Quin answers back, "Yes, of course, we think about that possibility. We had him down here last night, asking him about his whereabouts after leaving the hospital, and we wanted a look at his cell phone records."

"Yeah, I was very curious about that too. The part about where was he all that time I thought he was with you guys, the police, what did he have to say about that?"

"As you know firsthand, Mr. Hanson isn't much of a father, and his travels that evening were well documented. It seems Mr. Hanson makes a habit of hitting the strip-club circuit quite regularly, plus he knows some of the dancers firsthand."

"I don't mean to sound like a Boy Scout, but explain to me what *firsthand* means."

Quin answers back with a bit of disbelief in my question, "It means he goes out with them when they're not working, he has a key to two of the girls' apartments. That's where he went when he left the hospital. He told us just to take a shower and get some rest before he went back to your place to pick up his daughter. After all, it was getting late, and he said the kid was probably asleep anyway, why bother her? That guy is always thinking what's best for the kid, isn't he?"

"Oh yeah, that guy's a real peach," I reply.

Quin slips up for a second by saying, "OK, Bill," then corrects herself. "Mr. Mathews, let's head over to your place so we can get some things to bring back for forensics to check out." When I hear that, I push my chair back away from the desk, I stand and say, "I'll see you there," and with that, I turn and head for the elevator. I'm pissed, but just before I grab the doorknob to let myself out, I hear the sweet voice that says, "You have a nice day now, young man." I turn and see Officer Grandma with the most sincere smile, and I give her my best fake smile back and say, "Thank you, Officer, see you again," and made my exit.

I was home almost an hour before Quin shows up. She pulls her unmarked car into my driveway. She's got some young uniformed cop sitting in the passenger seat; he looks like he's straight-out of the academy, no more than twenty-one or twenty-two years old. She says, "Hope you don't mind me parking in your driveway?"

"And if I did?"

She says, "Then I guess I'd move it. Do you want me to move it?" she asks."

"No, I don't want you to move it, just do what you gotta do and then you can move it for good."

"You sound a little uptight there, Bill." This time she let the first name stand.

"Yeah, you could say that, but I'm more upset with myself than you, I'm the one who put myself in this spot." I say, "Come with me, I'll let you in the house."

"Thank you, this is Cadet Jensen." As Quin gently grabs the kid by the bicep and gives him a slight nudge in my direction, I don't offer him my hand to shake; I just nod my head to acknowledge his presence. I hold the front door open and let the both of them enter the house first; I then ask, "Where do you want to start first?"

Quin says, "We want all your shoes, you can keep slippers if you have those. But we want the shoes you have on now, plus the clothes you were wearing the night you went into the Hansons' backyard. We know pretty much what they looked like, the police officer stationed in front of the house told us what he saw that night."

"Yeah, I know. You can have my whole wardrobe if you want."

"No, that won't be necessary. We know what we're looking for, and that's all we want today." As Quin and I are talking, the kid cop is walking into my bedroom with several evidence bags. He's only in there four or five minutes, and he comes back out with pants, shoes, and shirts and then looks at me and opens a bag in front of me and looks down at my feet and says, "We need those, remember?"

"Yes, I remembered." So I head over to my recliner and remove my shoes and hand them over for him to drop into the bag, and then he sealed the bag and wrote something down on the bag itself. Then the kid says, "Detective O'Hara, I noticed a flashlight in his room, would you like me to get that?"

"Yes, Ryan, that might be useful, you never know." So he took out a small bag from his pocket and headed back into my room.

"Is that going to be all?" I asked, "or do you want me to give you a blood sample?"

"No, that might come later during the investigation, but thanks for offering," she quipped.

After she said that, I kept thinking, *The more I try to be cute, the more I sound like a jerk.* With that thought in my head, the phone rang. I went over an answered it, and on the other end is a little kid's voice, asking, "Is this Bill?" I'm confused.

I say, "Yes, who is this?"

"It's Maggie, don't you recognize my voice?"

"No, not really," I say. "I've never talked to you on the phone before, and how did you get my phone number?"

"I guess you gave it to my dad? He was the one who gave it to me."

"Oh well, it doesn't matter how you got it, I'm just glad you called. How are you doing anyway?"

"Oh, I guess I'm doin' OK. Gramma's crying all the time, I kinda take care of her, she's so sad."

"Maggie, you never cease to amaze me, you're wise above your years. But why did you call. You want to set a date to go to lunch?"

"No, that's not why I called. I called to tell you the funeral is going to be this Thursday, and I want you to come. Will you please come, Bill?"

"Yes, I promise I'll be there. I will get the information, and I'll be there promise, but right now I got to go. I have Detective Quin here asking me questions."

"Oh, tell her hi for me. I like her."

"OK, I will. Gotta go, talk to you later. Bye."

As soon as I hang up, I turn to the direction of Quin and relay the message. "That was Maggie, and she wanted me to say hello and she likes you, the rest of the conversation was for me."

"Well, that's nice, I like her too, be sure and tell her that the next time you see or talk to her. As far as what we needed from you, I think we have everything. We'll be on our way. Good day, Mr. Mathews." And with that, she and her sidekick were out the door and gone. As I watched them drive off down the street, I couldn't help but notice a black and white unit was at the Hanson's' place, removing the yellow tape from around the house. And thinking to myself as I was walking back into the house, *I wonder if Roger will be coming back to the house. And if he does, would he take a chance and bring one of his playmates for a sleepover? I know he's a creep, but come on, would he dare take that kind of a risk? One of the neighbors could easily spot him, maybe the word could get out, "He killed for love, not money." It happens all the time in husband-and-wife killings. Maybe he was tired of being a husband and dad, maybe he just wanted to go back to his single, play-the-field days, a new girl every week.* I was also thinking, *I wonder if Maggie was supposed to stay home when he went out to the bakery. Maybe she begged, "Please, Daddy, let me go, please. I want to pick something special for Mommy, please. And with that, he was forced to take her with him. I don't know, I just have all these thoughts going through my mind. I wish I didn't get off to such a terrible start with Detective Quin, I would love to share my thoughts with her. But I do have an idea. Since the crime tape is down at Roger's place, I think that means the house, and what happened in it, is now public record. I not only could get a copy of the police report, I could also get a printout of the autopsy. Yeah, I can do that and see how my theory stacks up to the police findings. I'm almost sure I can do this because of the Freedom of Information Act. I'm going to call Quin and check with her. If I don't like her answer, I will call over to the records department. I will get those reports for that, I am sure.*

I went and got a notepad. I wanted to start writing down my thoughts when they were fresh in my mind, and not only my thoughts of how the murder was committed, but also how Roger could be involved. When it came to the slaying, my feelings were

Maggie's mother was grabbed from behind in a choke hold and was overpowered and was repeatedly stabbed in the chest, with some of the stabs reaching the heart. The whole attack shouldn't have lasted more than one or two minutes. The thing I don't understand is why there was no blood on the patio door; the killer had too have gotten blood on the hand that did the stabbing; I doubt the killer took time to wash up in the sink. But when I get that police report, I'll be able to see what they found at the scene. It only took me an hour or so, and I had my notes all in order. I was on the phone setting up a meeting with my favorite homicide detective, Quin O'Hara.

In no time, I was on the phone, and actually kind of excited with anticipation to discuss my investigation prowess with a real, live homicide detective. This time I got her and not voice mail; as soon as she finished her introduction, I said, "Hello, Detective, this is Bill Mathews, and I need to set up a meeting with you, and I will be glad to come "downtown". That's what they say in the movies, you know what I mean?"

"Yes, Mr. Mathews, I watch TV. I know what you mean." I don't know if she could tell in my voice or not, but I was almost giddy with excitement. I wanted so much to share my thoughts and hunches with her; I respected her as a competent and intelligent detective, plus she wasn't too hard to look at either. She says, "When do you plan on coming downtown, Mr. Mathews?"

"Hey, I'm in the car now."

"Very well. I will see you shortly." She then hangs up without another word. I'm thinking, *That was kind of rude, but then again, what else was there for her to say? Maybe something like, "OK, Bill, I'll wait right here at my desk until you get here, can't wait to see you." Yeah,* I thought, *that would have been much better.* Then I also thought, *I do have a very active imagination.*

Before I knew it, I was standing in the lobby of the Riverside Police Department. This time, as I was waiting for the elevator, my stomach was calm and still, much different than just a few hours ago. As I reached the second floor, I was ready to do battle with Quin if necessary. I opened the door to the homicide department office and was immediately surprised to hear, "It's you again, back so soon? I bet you're here again to see Detective O'Hara, am I right?"

It was the sweet, grandmotherly officer, all smiles, like she really was glad to see me again. I said, "Why yes, I am."

"You know you're quite the detective yourself." She gave out a chuckle and said, "You know where she's at, I'll let you go alone this time." I gave her a sincere smile this time and headed back toward Quin's desk. She was sitting as I approached her, and she said, "Please have a seat." This time she said neither Bill nor Mr. Mathews. I couldn't get any vibes off her, good, bad, or indifferent. I opened up with both barrels so to speak. I said, "Quin, I have some very educated theories on this murder, and I would like to see the police report and a copy of the autopsy on this case." She used both hands on her desk to push herself away; the wheels hit carpet or something because her chair came to an abrupt stop, and she said in a bit higher-pitched voice, "You want what?" I thought, *She will not intimidate me.*

I came back with, "You heard me, do we have a problem with my request? And may I say, it's a request now, but I could demand if that's necessary, but I don't want to do that. I would very much like to work with you on the solving of this case."

"Mr. Mathews." She paused, took a big sigh, and continued. "Don't you understand this is an ongoing active case?"

I say, "Whoa, the police have removed the crime tape from the house, people are free to come and go inside that house. Am I right? Also, the body has been cleared to be buried, is that right?" Before she can answer, I answer for her, "Yes, that's right, and I know I have every right to review those reports because that's the law. Detective O'Hara. I came in peace; I came with ideas; I came to try and assist you in finding who killed little Maggie's mother, why do you fight me every step of the way? Doesn't the saying go 'Two heads are better than one?' I know I did screw up when I went back into the crime area, but can't we get over that and try and work as a team?"

"OK, let's hold on for a minute," she says, "let's back up. You came, as you called it, *downtown*." She used the two-little-fingers-thing to illustrate quotes for *downtown*, which made me smile and, in turn, did the same for her. "So let's you and I start talking about what you saw and what you suspect."

I say "You're right," and from that point on, all was smooth sailing. She told me about Roger's phone records, before the killing and after the killing; she also told me there was no extra life insurance bought, and what they had was just about enough to pay for the funeral. He didn't spend more time with one girl over another; in other words, he didn't seem to have a favorite. Quin also did some checking up on all the girls Roger had dated, trying to find out where they all were at the time of the killing. They all had solid alibis for that dreadful Sunday morning. Roger didn't have any money; he couldn't have paid anyone to do it. After hearing all about Roger and his secret lifestyle, his meager job with an average income, I thought, *What a waste, he had a very attractive wife, a great kid, and they were happy with him, just as he was. But that life was too vanilla for Roger, he wanted that free swinger life, the one with no wife, no kids, the kind you could come and go as you please. Who knows, maybe those girls were taking care of him?* But the more I kept thinking back to the morning he and Maggie came to my door, I think it was real fear and concern I saw in his face. In short, I have come to the decision that Roger is too wimpy too have had any part in his wife's murder. I think Quin was ahead of me dropping Roger as a suspect. I thought all had gone very well. You know, the two of us comparing notes so to speak. That was until I brought up the autopsy; she said, "Are you sure you think you're entitled to see those reports?" I say in my calmest voice, "Yes, yes, I am, it's called the Freedom of Information Act. She, I believe mocking me, uses her almost whisper voice and says, "Yes, I know what it's called."

"OK then," I say, "what's the problem?" She then begins to stand up and says, "You wait right here, I am going to speak with my supervisor about your request." I say, "Sure, no problemo. I'll be right here when you come back."

As I sat and waited for her return, I told myself not to waver on my demands; as she came back, she didn't give any indication that she was upset or put out but a gaze of dissuasion. She didn't bother to sit back down; she knew our day was over. She said, "You can pick up a copy of both the police report and the autopsy tomorrow morning at the county clerk's office. That'll be at courthouse, even further downtown, and with that information, I think our day is done, Mr. Mathews." I got the message loud and clear; she was not at all happy with me sticking my nose in her job. I could kind of see her point; it's like I was looking over her shoulder, but my feelings weren't hurt, and I said my thanks and was headed home.

On my way home, my thoughts went back to my little buddy Maggie. I had to admit I missed her. After I got back to my place, I gave her a call; it was a good thing I had that caller ID thing because I never asked for her number when she called me, telling me about the funeral. I called and got an elderly woman who answered. I explained who I was and asked if she was Maggie's grandmother. She said yes, and I told her how sorry I was about the loss of her child. She thanked me for my kind thoughts and said she would go track down Mags. It wasn't but a half minute and she was on the other end, saying, "Is this you, Bill?" And she said it with real, honest-to-goodness joy. It made me warm inside; I never knew what that expression meant before. Not until that moment. I said, "Yes, Mags, it's me, and I want you to ask your grams if I can come over now and we can go out for an early dinner, and we will go wherever you want, I'll let you pick." Maggie was quick to reply, "The last time we went out to eat, I got to pick the place. I say this time it's your choice, after all, you're the one picking up the check."

"Right," I say, "right, but the guy's almost always supposed to do that."

She says, "I guess, hold on, I'll go ask Grams if I can go, she might already have plans for us, plus my aunt Barbara is here, so hold on, I'll be right back." And with that, I could hear the receiver being set down and the muffled sound of Maggie calling out for her grandmother.

It became completely quiet for a while, then the voice of Maggie's grandmother came on the line. "Hello again, this is Mrs. Knowland, Maggie's grandmother. Maggie seems to have quite a fondness for you Mister – " She paused, "Oh, I'm sorry, I don't know your last name. Maggie refers to you as Bill."

I said, "It's Mathews, but I would like to be called Bill if that's all right with you, Mrs. Knowland."

"Well, for right now, until I know you better, I feel more comfortable referring to you as Mr. Mathews, I hope you understand."

"Oh yes, I completely understand your position."

"Well, Mr. Mathews, let me get straight to the point, you see, we have never met, and I don't feel very comfortable letting my granddaughter go out alone with you. Roger seems to think you're all right, but let's face it, Roger doesn't always make wise choices, not meaning that you're not an all-right gentleman, mind you."

I say, "Yes, I understand your position completely, Mrs. Knowland."

"But let me propose a solution if I may, Mr. Mathews."

I say, "Please do."

"You see, my younger daughter is here with me. She is trying to give me support through this most difficult time for me. Maggie is begging for my permission for her to go out with you for dinner. I say yes, it will be OK with me, on the condition that Barbara accompanies you. Oh, Does that meet your satisfaction, Mr. Mathews?"

"Why that will be fine. I will head over toward your place as soon as I get dressed. Just give me your address, *I misplaced the paper Roger gave me* and I'll see you in an hour and a half or so."

And with that, I was headed for my closet. I knew I didn't have a large variety to choose from, but that was no problem. I had a nice pair of dress slacks, a clean white shirt, and the jacket that went to my suit; I thought a tie would be a little too formal, so I threw that combination on and I was ready. I did one more look over, liked what I saw, and was off. I remember Roger or someone telling me the house was about forty-five minutes out of town, so without me getting lost on the way, I should be there right on schedule. As I turned onto the designated street, I slowed down, checking each house number as I crawled by. I found the number on the curb; the corresponding ones on the houses were too hard to read due to the fact that the houses were set so far back from the actual street. These houses were large and had private driveways up to their front door; these were the kind of houses you would see in those old black and white movies you'd see from the forties. I drove up to the front; it had a wide front porch, with an equally wide concrete stairway leading up to it. I parked the car right in front of the steps; before I could get myself completely out of the car, I was greeted with a wonderful-sounding young child's voice.

"Bill, you made it." Before I could get myself out of the car, she was at my side. She had a genuine smile, a smile that said "Bill, I'm happy to see you" and "Bill, I'm happy you're here." As I got out of the car, she took me by my hand and said, "I want you to meet my aunt Barbara." As I looked up in the direction of the front door, I saw her; she was standing in the open doorway. I don't know if it was the setting sun or light from inside the house, but whatever caused it made her look like a glowing or radiant angel. She looked like she was in her late twenties, with blond hair and what I would call a perfect figure. As I walked up the steps, I had to make sure I didn't fall or stumble; I couldn't take my eyes off her. I had to look down not only to see the steps but also not to embarrass myself from staring. She spoke first. "Hello, you must be Mr. Mathews," and with that, she offered her hand. I didn't say anything; I was still looking at her. She was about five-nine or five-ten, weighing in the range of 130 or 140 pounds, and fitting into a blue dress like nothing I had ever seen. Maggie's voice snapped me out of my trance. "Well, aren't you going to shake hands with my aunt Barbara, Bill?"

"Oh yes, of course, I'm sorry." And with that, our hands interlocked. I could feel the firm, strong, confident handshake of a remarkably beautiful woman, I did get out the words, "Please call me Bill." And that kind of surprised me because I thought I was going to be speechless.

She continues, "Well, I must say it's nice to be able to put a face to all we heard about you from, Mags. Please come in, my mother also wants to meet you." And with that, I was escorted into the house; we only got partway into the next room when Maggie let out a holler. "Hey, Grams, Bill is here, and it looks like he got all dressed up to meet you." That last part made me blush, and Aunt Barbara saw it and said, "Why, Bill, you're blushing," then followed that up with, "I think that's charming in a man." When she said that, that even made me blush all the more. But I must say, when she spoke my name, it made my heart skip a beat; I felt like I was a young schoolboy around my first real crush. Mrs. Knowland came into the room and looked nothing like any grandmother I ever remember; she was also a very attractive woman. I would say she was in her mid to late fifties but could pass for fortyish. She also held her hand out in greeting. For some reason, I had the urge to bend down and kiss her hand; of course, I didn't, but it ran across my mind. Again with the daydreaming stuff, I thought, *No wonder Maggie likes me, we both have the mind of a child.* Mrs. Knowland then says, "You kids better get going before it gets too late, and thank you for taking Barbs with you, I hope you don't mind and do understand my point of view."

"Yes, I understand completely, and yes, we should be on our way." And with that, we were loading into the car and on our way to dinner. As we were driving, I turned to Maggie in the backseat and said, "I made reservations for the Sherrington Hotel Restaurant, how does that sound to you, ladies?" Barbara spoke first while looking back at Maggie. "Oh, Mags, you're going to love it there. It's really nice, and they have the best salad and homemade bread."

Maggie says, "Aunt Barb, if you say it's nice, I believe it. You have been to so many fine restaurants, you know, the good ones."

I say, "It's good we have someone who knows the finer places."

Barb says, "Oh yes, I can tell you all the hot spots in all of Riverside." I look over at her and just smile.

In no time, I was handing over my keys to the valet parking lot attendant, a young man in a red bow tie and matching vest. He took my keys and handed me a ticket. Maggie asks, "Hey, Bill, what did that man give you?" I told her it was a claim check ticket for my car. I added, "That means, when we're done eating and we come out here to get my car, I give him that ticket, and he knows what car is mine and where it's parked."

She says, "Wow, that sounds pretty fancy, this must be a classy place."

"Well, I don't know about that, but I'm sure it's very nice, and as your aunt Barbara said, they have good salads and bread."

Barbara reaches over and pats Maggie on the head and says, "I think you'll like it very much." I hold open one-half of two very large glass doors, and we enter into a large foyer.

The foyer is encircled with large flowerless potted plants; also, there was another set of large glass doors, but unlike the other set of doors, these were being held open by a young man, this time wearing a black bow tie with matching vest. As we enter into a very large room with beautiful overhead lighting and large columns interlacing the room, giving the appearance of holding up the ceiling, I was now feeling the same way Maggie was. Wow, this is a fancy place. The only one not looking at the ceiling in awe was Barbara, but that made sense; she had been here before. The receptionist said, "Good evening, what's the name on the reservation?" I stepped to the podium and said, "Mathews." The receptionist then turned, stood up, and raised her hand and got the attention of the head waiter; he stopped what he was doing and came directly to us. He looked at me and said, "Please follow me." He took us to a nice table; he noticed it was a table with four chairs and asked, "Are you expecting another guest?"

I said, "No, it's just the three of us," but before he could get the attention of a bus boy, I told him, "You can leave the extra chair, it will be fine." He then held the chairs out for the girls and left us with three large dinner menus. Maggie didn't even open it; she was looking all over the restaurant. She was in total amazement of her surroundings.

I said, "Hey, Mags, what do you think of this place?" She looked at me and said, "Bill, I think only millionaires come here, it's so magnificent."

Barbara then spoke up. "Maggie, let me tell you, this is a nice place, but it's a far cry from a millionaires' club. Just look around, it's just regular people like you and me and Bill."

I then speak up. "I'm glad you like it, and as far as I'm concerned, we fit in very nicely. Now let's see if we can find something we can eat and have a real nice evening out." Maggie says, "Yes, you're right, Bill, and you can tell me what you saw in the kitchen."

I went, "Oh, I don't know if we should talk about that now."

Barbara says, "What are you guys talking about?" Maggie says, "Bill and I are trying to find out who killed my mom, we snuck into my backyard, and Bill looked into the kitchen with his flashlight."

Barbara looks at me with amazement. "You're kidding me, aren't you?"

"No, I wish I was because I got myself in a heap of trouble with the police."

"How's that," asked Barbara.

Because I had to tell the lead detective about my sneaking around when she started asking me questions that I couldn't answer fast enough. I didn't want to start stammering, so I just told her what I did and came clean with her." Maggie seemed to forget about her surroundings and looked across the table at me and, with great concern in her face, asked me, "Are you in bad trouble, Bill?"

"Mags, I gotta tell you the truth, I'm in trouble, that's for sure. I just don't know how much, but let's not worry about that now. Let's order dinner, I'm starving."

Barbara then says, "Bill's right, let's not discuss that kinda stuff tonight, let's enjoy this magnificent restaurant and one another's company."

With that, the rest of the evening was uneventful, and that was fine with me. My main concern leading up to the night out was how I was going to explain my findings at the Hansons' place to my dear little newest best friend, and you know, she forgot all about asking me anything when she thought I might be, as she said, in big trouble. After I dropped off Mags with Aunt Barbara, I went straight home. I was beat, but not tired enough to get Barbara off my mind. She was, without a doubt, a very sexy woman, one I wanted to see more of, which would be tomorrow at the funeral.

I turned off the lights and was headed for bed, but a little flashing light caught my eye; I very seldom get phone messages, so it was out of the ordinary to see that light blinking the way it was. I was curious to see who it could be. I pushed the button and waited with interest. "Hello, Mr. Mathews, this is Detective O'Hara." As soon as I heard her introduction, I knew she was all business. She continued, "I would like to see you in my office tomorrow, I know the funeral is also tomorrow, and I plan on attending, but I want to keep myself in the background, so I would prefer you don't acknowledge me at the cemetery, so if you would, please meet me between two and three p.m. Thank you." Sound of receiver being set down. I thought, *Wow, that's not going to help me get a good night's sleep.* With that, I was off to bed. I had to admit it, I was very concerned about why she wanted me at her office. I knew one thing; she didn't want to discuss the weather.

I tossed and turned throughout the night, but I was still glad when the morning arrived. I kept thinking, what did Quin want to talk about? All through my shower, my shaving, and getting dressed, I couldn't shake the feeling that I was somehow in more trouble than I wanted to think about. But first, I had to be there for my little sidekick; I know she had her grandmother, but she would be in no shape herself. Her aunt would be of some comfort, but I don't know how close they really were. Her dad would be of very little value, so I wanted to be there. If she needed me for a hug or a shoulder to cry on, I was going to be there. I would deal with my own problems after I took care of Mags. I fixed myself a cup of coffee, made sure I had the correct tie for a funeral, and was ready to head for the church.

The traffic was light this time of the day, so I was pulling into the church parking lot in no time flat. I had no trouble finding a parking spot. I was one of the first people there, I stayed in the car and waited for more cars to pull in. I was not anxious to go inside. I used to attend church quite regularly as a boy and young man, but I seemed to slip away from attending church as I got older. I would guess that's quite common with most adults my age. I could see the church was starting to fill quite rapidly, so I checked myself one last time in the rearview mirror and was out of the car. I made myself through the group of people standing and talking at the base of the stairway in front of the church, the women all dressed in black and all about the same age. As I excused myself for walking through, I thought, *These must be girls Mag's mother went to school with.* All the young men looked very successful and talked about who could have done such a terrible thing.

As I walked up the steps, the groups' conversations started to fade to a murmur. My mind started to drift again; I thought the murderer could be one of those guys I walked past in front of the church. But before my imagination got going full speed, I said, *Slow down*, then I drew my attention to finding a seat near the back. I figured the friends and relatives of the family should get the seats nearer the front. As I sat down, the first thing I did was look for Maggie; I wanted to see her demeanor. I saw her; she was in the first row. She was sitting with her father on one side and her grandmother on the other; next to her grandmother was Barbara, then next to her was an older man. Guessing by the color of his hair, I would say early to mid-sixties. I didn't know what part he played, but he must be family of some kind. I thought maybe it's Barbara's husband. After all, I didn't know that much about her, then I noticed three young women sitting behind the family; they were even younger than the group that was in front of the church when I came in. These girls looked like they were in their late teens or at most, twenty-one or twenty-two years old. They didn't have a clue on how to dress for a funeral; two of them had bright-colored low-cut tops, and I could imagine what the skirts looked like. The other sitting almost directly behind the gray-haired man was wearing what looked like a white two-piece business suit. I don't think the three of them were together, but they sure made a strange trio.

The service went along very smoothly; between, the preacher – or priest, I don't know which is which – asked the people, "Would any of you like to say a few words about your relationship with the departed, Mrs. Audrey Hanson?" And as I had guessed, some of the young women that were dressed in black spoke of their days taking turns being one another's bridesmaids. It was sad to think someone so young and so full of life and happiness could have an enemy that disliked her so much, they wanted her dead. The service was just about to end when I saw Maggie's father stand up. I thought, Oh *brother, what is he going to say?* But I was wrong. It wasn't Roger who was going to speak; it was Maggie. Roger had stood up to help her up to the pulpit and adjust the microphone for her. I stood up; I wanted her to see me if she looked out across the church. I wanted her to know I was listening and I was there for her. The church became eerily quiet; she strained too get close to speak into the mic; her little child's voice echoed throughout the church. "I want to thank everyone for coming today. It shows me my mommy had lots of friends. She had people other than me and my grandma, my aunt Barbara, and my dad that loved her like we did. I also want to say the police and other people I know will find the person who killed my mother, and I'm making that promise in the church, and that means I'm going to keep it." And with that, she stepped away from the pulpit and was met by her dad, and they sat back down. The church now had a chorus of whispers throughout. I was proud of my sidekick. She was not only one smart little cookie, I also just found out she was a tough one too. With that, the preacher thanked everyone for coming and told everyone there would be a motorcade leaving for the grave site shortly.

I drifted out of the church, didn't see a soul I knew, and made it to my car nonstop. I sat in the car and just watched all the people walk past my car, absolutely oblivious to me. I wondered, *Has the murderer just walked by my car?* Before long, the cars all started to move out; there was a motorcycle cop directing traffic out of the lot and onto the main drag. As I pulled into the procession, I noticed how large a group had attended the service. We meandered through city streets for about twenty minutes then found ourselves going through a gated cemetery. I pulled over and parked almost as soon as we entered the archway gates. Again, I wanted the family and friends to be able to park closer to the grave site. I locked the car and started to walk; the cars kept streaming in behind me. I was thinking about Maggie's words when I was grabbed by the arm. It startled me; I turned quickly, only to see Quin. I said, "I see you made it."

She said back. "I told you I was going to make it and remain in the background," and then she says, "It looks like your keeping a low profile yourself."

I say, "No, I just parked far away. When I get up toward the grave, I'll let Maggie see me. In fact, I want her to see me. So tell me, Detective, were you at the church when Maggie spoke?"

"No, I wasn't, what did she have to say?"

"She said the police and others would catch the killer of her mom."

"And I presume you would be *others*?" Quin asks me. "Yes, I would think that would be me. Maggie has faith in me, she thinks I can be a great asset to the police." I excuse myself from Quin when I see Maggie waving and running in my direction. Maggie shows signs of heavy crying. I bend down with open arms for her arrival. Before she can speak, I tell her how proud I was of her, but I don't think she heard a word I said; she just zoomed in and landed her head on my shoulder. She didn't whimper or cry; she just said, "I'm so glad you're here, please sit with me and Grams."

I was the one who started to stammer and stutter. "Gee, I don't know about that, kid, that's where the family sits. I wouldn't feel right being there. I'll tell you what I will do. I'll get up in the front and stand off to one side, right next to the tent."

"OK, I guess that'll be fine, but I want to talk to you before you go home."

I say, "Yes, I promise I won't leave until I talk with you." We then made our way up to the grave site; she broke away, following her grandmother's hand signals, and I slipped in next to the approaching preacher then backed up a bit when we were directly at the tent.

I made it look like I was part of the cemetery staff; now I was in a position where I could see Grandma Knowland, Aunt Barbara, the grieving husband, Maggie, and the gray-haired mystery man; the two young girls with the revealing blouses were nowhere to be seen, but the other young and attractive female in the business suit was located again directly behind the gray-haired gentleman. Maggie saw me and gave me a little wave of her hand while her hand remained on her lap. She was very discreet.

From my point of view, I could see everything, and the things I noticed were very interesting. First, I could see the agony that Mrs. Knowland was going through; it was downright pain in her face. Next to her was her youngest child, Barbara, and Barbara was doing her best to comfort her mother, using one hand to hold her mother's hand and gently patting her back with the other, all the time whispering something or humming a lullaby. I couldn't make that part out, but the point was she was trying to keep her mom calm. Then there was Roger sitting next to Maggie; he had a handkerchief in his hand, and he was crying real tears; he also looked shaken and truly sad. I noticed Maggie patting her dad's leg, trying to ease his pain; and the way I saw it, his sorrow was real. Then after a few comforting taps on his leg, he realized the taps of comfort were coming from his daughter, a daughter who had just lost her mother; he looked over to Maggie and then put his arm around her shoulders and pulled her very tightly next to him, and with that, Maggie dropped her head on her dad's lap and wept. I started to feel my own tears rolling down my cheeks; I was so happy that Roger snapped out of his own grief and gave fatherly attention and love to his little daughter. I whispered to myself, "Thank you God." Now my focus turned to the gray-haired man; at the church, I could only see the back of his head, but now I could see a very well-kept middle-aged man. By the looks of his suit and shoes, I would say a very well-to-do middle-aged man. Since I was only a few feet away from the entire family, I could see that the gray-haired man was downright weak with grief himself. This was no friend of the family or a close uncle; no, it was plain as day. Now that I saw him and his head down and his entire upper torso sagging, this is the same kind of pain Mrs. Knowland displayed; this man had to be Maggie's Grandfather.

It all made complete sense now, but I would guess that Mr. Knowland was pretty much out of the everyday life of the Hanson family. Barbara didn't show much attention to her dad throughout the day, so I would say they weren't close either. The preacher asked for everyone to stand as he gave his final prayers over the open grave. Most bowed their heads, while others were headed for their cars; the prayer was short, and the service was complete. Maggie headed in my direction with Aunt Barb in tow right behind her.

Maggie was almost cheerful as she approached me. She said, almost matter-of-factly, "Aren't you glad this day is almost over with?"

I tell her, "Yes, I'm glad it's almost over for you."

Barbara then speaks up, "Maggie and I would like to invite you over to the house, that would be my mother's house, of course, for some refreshments." Before I could give her an answer, I was gently tapped on the shoulder. Before I could turn to see who did the tapping, I heard a very familiar voice, reminding me of a previous appointment. It was Detective Quin. She said hello to Maggie and told her how sorry she was about losing her mother then offered her hand to Barbara, saying, "I don't believe we have ever met, I'm Quin," leaving out the *detective* part."

"Oh, it's very nice too meet you, I'm Maggie's aunt, Barbara. Audrey was my sister."

Quin comes back with, "Oh, I'm so sorry, this is such a sad day, one that should have never taken place, and it all seems so senseless."

Barbra then says, "I was just telling Mr. Mathews, I mean, Bill, about a little get-together over at my mother's. We would love to have you, would you please join us?" And before Quin could answer, Maggie is pleading, "Yes, please come over to Gram's house, please, I would really like that."

Quin now turns back to me and says, "You do remember we have an appointment this afternoon?"

I say, "Yes, of course, how could I ever forget something like that." I then put the ball in her court; I say, "Can we go over too Maggie's for a bite to eat then have our meeting afterward? I'll do whatever you want, you make the call." Before she can give an answer, Maggie is holding her hands in a praying position and pleading Quin to "Please come over, even if it's just an hour or so."

Quin concedes and says "OK, just an hour, no more. I have lots of work to do back at the office." Mags is happy, and we all head off to our cars. Mrs. Knowland's house isn't that far from the cemetery, and before you knew it we were all pulling into the Knowland driveway almost simultaneously.

Barbara and Maggie were the first ones headed into the house. As they went through the standing open doors, Maggie took a peek back, looking for someone. I'm thinking it was the combo of Quin and myself. Mags got a glimpse of the two of us and let out a wave acknowledging our attendance. Quin and I waved back in unison. As we entered the house, you couldn't help but notice a very long table filled with a very large assortment of food; also off to the side was a small bar with a female attendant serving up drinks. The bar was a very popular spot; it was three or four deep. Everyone needed a drink after such an emotional day.

I thought, *You know, a drink does sound pretty good right about now, but I have never been one who likes any kind of lines.* I wouldn't care if they were giving away brand-new five-dollar bills; I was not standing in any line. Now if we're talkin' hundreds, where's the line form? So I guess I considered a drink about the same as a free fiver. Barbara sees my dilemma and says, "Hey, Bill, you come with me and I'll take you where there are no lines, and you, Detective, can I get you a drink?"

Quin answers in a very polite reply, "Oh, no thank you, technically, I'm on duty, but please, you guys go ahead, and I don't blame you a bit." And with that, we were ushered into a very large and spacious kitchen. There was an island in the middle of the room filled with liquor bottles of every imaginable choice, a bucket of ice, and several choices of mix. I guess they expected an overflowing crowd at the dining room bar and had this little hideout for the VIP.

Maggie asked her aunt, "Would it be all right if I show Quin and Bill my room?"

Barb says, "I don't see why not."

With that, Maggie says, "Come on, fix your drink and bring it with you. Remember, we haven't got all day."

Barbara tells Mags, "You take Detective Quin, and I will bring up Bill as soon as I fix his drink for him, is that OK?"

"Yeah, but don't take forever," and with those parting words, Mags and Quin, hand in hand, were off.

As soon as Quin and Mags were out of earshot, Barbs asks, "Are you in trouble with the police because of that entering-the-crime-scene stunt you pulled?"

"Yeah, I kinda think I am, plus I've been requesting police reports and such, and that also has pissed them off a bit." Barbs takes a step backward, puts both of her hands on her hips, and says, "You gotta be kiddin'?"

I come right back and say, "Don't get all wound up, it's the law, I have every right to see all the stuff they have on file, and let's not talk about it now. I'm on the clock, and I would like that drink before I have to meet up with Quin."

Barb says, "Sorry, you're right, what can I fix you?"

"Just give me a tall screwdriver and light on the ice."

She replies, "Sounds good, I'll have one with you, and we better get upstairs before Maggie starts screaming, 'What's taking you guys so long?'" So two large drinks were made very fast and very strong. We made our way to Mags's room. Before she let out any hollers, we walked into the room; we found Mags and Quin sitting on the edge of her bed. Maggie was showing Quin a photo album. Mags stopped turning the pages and said, "Hey, Bill, come sit next to me, I want to show you some pictures of me and my mom when I was small." Barbara motions me over in the direction of her niece and says, "You go look, I've already seen them." As I sit down next to my little partner, she says, "This is my stuff," lifting up the photo album. "Almost everything in this room Grams has gotten for me. This room has got more great stuff than my room at home, that's because Grams spoils me. I'll show you my special things another time. Right now, I want you to see how beautiful my mom was." And with that last comment, I sat myself down next to Mags.

The photos looked like they had spanned the last four or five years. And Mags was right on the money with her description of her mother; indeed, she was a beauty. There were pictures from Christmas, birthdays, and the general selections that bring families together. I couldn't help but notice the lack of Granddad and Aunt Barbara in the family pics. I was looking for Barb in the photo when everyone was poolside. I saw the late Audrey in a two-piece bathing suit, and I must say she was very impressive to say the least. I scanned the whole page, trying to see Barb in her swimming wear, but no luck. I even brought it up, asking, "Hey, Aunt Barb, I don't see you anywhere here poolside." I even came right out and said, "I would have loved to see you in your bathing attire."

"Oh, you'll have to wait a while for that, I'm not much of a sun person, I burn very easily."

"Oh, that's too bad was" my weak response. As the pages from the photo album slowly turned, I was always trying to catch a glimpse of the very beautiful and sexy Aunt Barbara, but very rarely was she in the shot. Finally, I spoke up and said, "Where are you in all these family functions?"

"Oh, believe me, I would have loved to have been at all the family gatherings, but my job has me working the craziest hours, and with lack of seniority, I always get the holiday shifts." Barb seems very emotional when explaining her absence. I had to ask, "Just what kind of job do you have?" She then very proudly says, "I work at the hospital, I'm a nurse and I love my job, but because of my occupation, I miss a lot of family functions."

"Well, that's a real bummer" is my thoughtful answer to the problem.

"Yes," Barb says, "I think you pretty well summed up my feelings on the matter." Quin then spoils the atmosphere even further by telling me to "Drink up, we have a meeting to attend."

"Oh, by all means, let me slam the rest of this drink, and I will follow you to your office."

Maggie says, "The next time you guys come, I want to show you some real cool stuff."

"OK, OK, and next time, I won't be in a rush, will I, Detective?"

"Oh, I'm sure next time I won't be here, and you can make a whole day of it, Mr. Mathews."

Maggie is quick to reply, "Does that mean you're not coming back ever to see me, Quin?"

"No, it just means Bill, I mean Mr. Mathews, will be able to come and see you before I'll have a chance to. Remember, my job is to find out who harmed your mom. And I will work as long and as hard as I have to get them. This is my promise to you ,your grandma, dad, and aunt Barbara here. In fact, I want to promise everyone in this city, I will catch whoever did this crime."

Hearing this deep and somewhat poetic promise, Maggie jumps up and gives Quin a big hug around her waist. Quin, in turn, pats Maggie very softly on the top of her head. "Maggie, I have got to go now. I have so much paperwork stacked up on my desk. I need to get back and start working on it, and Mr. Mathews can help me, so that's why we need to be getting along." So Quin then made the gesture with her one hand, as a doorman would, showing me the door. I went over to Maggie, knelt down on both knees, and gave her a hug with a bit of a squeeze to it. I told her, "I am so proud of you, I just can't tell you enough." She said, "Bill, you will come back and see me again, won't you?"

"Yes, we would like that," Barbara adds in. I look up from my kneeling position right into eye contact with Barb and give an answer of "Yes, I'll be back to visit you both." Barbara then stoops down and puts her hand under one of my elbows and says, "Here, let me help you up, Bill." As I get to my feet, I see Quin standing in the doorway, pleading, "Can we please get going?"

I give a half smile and say, "You go, I will be right behind you, but I do want to say good-bye to Mrs. Knowland before we leave."

Quin says, "That won't be a problem, but you understand I don't want to spend all night at my desk."

"Yeah, yeah, I got it, I just want to let Mrs. Knowland know that I am sincerely sorry for her loss."

Quin says, "Do what you gotta do, I'm leaving. I hope to see you within the next thirty minutes sitting across from me at my desk, you got that?"

"Yes, I got that, and I will be there within thirty minutes. I give you my word."

Before I left the house, I did as I promised; I found Mrs. Knowland and told her how sorry I was and thanked her for her generous hospitality. From there I made a beeline for the police department and the desk of my favorite homicide detective, the divine Quin O'Hara. I was walking into her office well within the thirty-minute time limit. As I walked through the door, I was hoping to hear the friendly voice of my new friend, Officer Granma, but that wasn't to be. The receptionist's desk was vacant, so I made my way directly to the appointed rendezvous.

Quin was at her PC and never noticed me walking up to her desk. It wasn't until I pulled out the chair that she turned and saw me about to be seated; she took a quick glance at her watch and quickly replied, "I'm very impressed, you made it under thirty minutes."

"Yes, I told you I would. Now let's discuss this case. I have some theories, but I need those reports and the autopsy to confirm them."

"Yes, I have them right here for you." She then bends down and opens the bottom right-hand drawer and retrieves two manila folders. She then reaches across the desk to hand them to me. I thank her as I pull them from her grip. "Mr. Mathews, I would now like to ask you some questions."

"Sure, have at it."

"First, tell me, other than your residents and the Hanson place, where did you go the day of the murder?"

"Nowhere, that's it, oh no, I forgot about the hospital and the pizza parlor. But I was with Maggie all that time."

"Then could you tell me, did you change your clothes or shoes for any reason?"

"No, those are the same shirt, pants, and shoes I put on in the morning and the same ones I took off that evening. Oh, I forgot you and the rookie took my shoes with you, are you telling me you found blood or something on my shoes?"

"No, we didn't find any blood, but we did find traces of blue spunbonded polypropylene fibers."

"You say what? I have no idea what you just said. You found fibers, that much I got, but fibers of what, run that by me again."

"Yes, I'll be glad to, the fibers I'm talking about were found inside the house, but only in the attack area in the kitchen and on the outside step that leads into the kitchen through the sliding glass door."

"I have fibers because of my stupidity of walking through a crime scene. I can tell you I took evidence away with me, I did not bring it to the area."

"Mr. Matthews, that may be true, but how do we go about proving that?"

"I don't know. Give me a lie detector test!"

"That may take place down the line, but right now, do you have any questions for me?"

"Yes, I do, could you tell me the names and relationships of some of the people that were at the church?"

"Yes, we have a printout on most everyone that attended the service, do you have anyone in particular you want to know about?"

"Yes, I do, the older man that sat up front, I assume, was the father of the deceased."

"Yes, that was Mr. Knowland, anyone else you're interested in?"

"Yes, all the young girls that sat in the second row behind the family, there was one very well-dressed young lady, do you know where she fits into the picture?"

"Yes, we found out she works for Mr. Knowland as his personal secretary. She is more of a girlfriend type than an employee type, if you know what I mean."

"Yeah, I think I can put two and two together, but what about the other two girls, the ones in the short skirts and skimpy tops, where do they fit in? They never showed up on the grave site."

"Yes, we have someone watching Roger Hanson at all times. What we saw was Roger telling the two girls, which are two of his exotic-dancer girl friends, that they were out of place and not needed at any of the functions. It would be inappropriate. They seem to get the message and never attempted to attend the grave-site service." After Quin gave me the rundown on the women of interest, I fully understood how they fit into the overall picture.

I felt satisfied that these three young women had no reasonable reason to harm the young Mrs. Hanson, so I mentally crossed them off as potential suspects. But now I was anxious to read the police reports; I wanted to inspect them while I was still in the presence of Detective Quin so I could ask questions if I had any. So I came right out and asked, "How long will you be at your desk this afternoon?"

"I plan on being here for a few more hours, but why do you ask?"

"Because I would like to go over the police report with you and get your input.

"I don't think that will be possible today, Mr. Mathews. You must understand we have not ruled you out at this present time, so it would be improper to discuss any questions you may have at this time. I hope you understand my position."

"Yes, I guess I can, so in that case, I will be on my way, unless you need me for more questions?"

"No, that's it for right now, but please don't leave the area in case we need you at a later time."

"No, you don't have to worry about that. I will be at my place going over these reports you gave me, call me there if you need me for any reason." As I put my two hands on the edge of the desk to push my chair back and begin my assent to the standing position, the phone on the desk began to ring. Quin picked it up before a second ring took place and answered, "Yes, sir." There was a short pause then Quin looking directly at me and holding out her arm and extending the index finger in the air, indicating "one minute please," and closing the one-sided conversation with "Yes, I understand" then setting down the receiver ever so slowly on its base. "Well, Bill, that was my supervisor, and he told me you will have to get your lawyer or a court order to take those files home with you, so if you please," she said with her hand held out, "may I please have them back." Reluctantly, I handed them over, never even getting the chance to open them.

I immediately left the police station and made my way home; I felt confused and somewhat depressed. I asked myself, *Am I doing the right thing asking for police reports and such? Or should I just concentrate on clearing my name of this homicide?* The answer was simple – take care of myself first then try and be a junior detective and help solve the crime. But the way things were, going I think I needed a lawyer, and that would be first on my things-to-do list when I got home. As I pulled into my driveway, I noticed a very new model silver Corvette already parked in my spot. I coasted up into the open space next to it and looked over into the mystery car and saw a hand waving at me. I couldn't make out who it was due to the late-evening glare. I got myself out of my car and made my way to the driver's side of the Vette. As I was reaching for the door handle, the door swung open, and a pair of knockout legs made their way out, followed by the rest of the body that was connected to it. Wow, I was in awe; it took me a moment to look up for a face to go to the body. It was Barbara in all her glory.

I found myself standing there, holding the door handle, still transfixed on those legs. I willed my mouth to talk as my mind tried to process the pure delight of such an incredible sight. "What a nice surprise, how long have you been waiting?"

"Oh, not long at all, I knew you had that appointment with that detective."

"Quin."

"Yeah, that's her name, how did that go?"

"I'll tell you all about it, but let's go inside." I took one of her hands and guided her the rest of the way out of the low seat of the Corvette. "Why thank you, Bill, you're quite the gentleman."

"No, not really, I'd use any excuse to be able to hold your hand."

"Boy, what a charmer you turned out to be" was Barb's immediate response.

I came back with "Please, let's get in the house where I can really dazzle you." I led her into the house, and before I asked her to be seated, I asked her if I could fix her anything. She said, "Maybe a little later, but right now, I'm interested on how your interview went."

"You mean the one with Detective Quin?"

"Yes, that's the one."

"Well, in my mind, it didn't go well at all. They had no sooner handed me the reports I requested than they turned around and demanded them back then told me I may need a court order to get them back."

"So you're telling me you came away empty-handed?"

"Yep, that would sum it up, but on the plus side, I'm not being held as the prime suspect of the murder of your sister."

"Yes, I guess I would consider that a plus also. Well, if you're OK, and it seems you are, so I'll be on my way."

"Hey, wait a minute, you just got here, what about that drink?"

"Well, Bill, as the saying goes, I'll take a rain check on that."

"OK, just remember, there will be no expiration date for the offer."

"That's sweet" was her answer. I thought, *What a bitch. I'll be dammed if I walk her to her car.* Holding the door open for her exit was the extent of my gentlemanly ways. As she brushed next to me, I just said "Have a good evening" and closed the door behind her. I thought as I stood there, still holding on to the doorknob, *What the hell just took place here?* I walked into the kitchen to fix myself a drink. *I don't get it, she is waiting in my driveway for I don't know how long then spends five minutes and splits. I don't think I'll ever figure out women.* But after my second drink, Barbara was completely out of my thoughts; my thoughts were on my obtaining those reports. It may come to the point that they may not help me solve the crime but to help eliminate me. I think that was my objective now. As I started on my third drink, I came to the conclusion I was done; I had hit the proverbial wall. I was so tired I unconsciously threw my almost full drink down the sink instead of putting it into the fridge for another day. That's when I headed straight for the bed and would tackle all my obstacles in the dawn of a new day.

And that new day greeted me as sliver-sized sun rays escaped through my window blinds. I was somewhat surprised how refreshed I felt. I thought that due too so much on my mind, I would toss and turn and wake up several times during the night, but that was not the case; I slept like a rock, thank the Lord. I was making my way into the kitchen for my morning coffee when the silence of the empty house was shattered by the sound of a telephone ring; it sounded extra loud and even more annoying than usual. As I stepped through the doorjamb of the kitchen entrance, I looked up at the wall clock located above the sink, wondering who would be calling at such an early hour. I saw it was 6:45 a.m., so I thought it must be somewhat urgent. I grabbed it before another ring could repeat itself and said "Hello," then I waited with interest for the voice to respond to my hello.

"Good morning, Bill, sorry to call so early, but I thought you would like to hear what I have to offer you."

I said, "Sure, but you'll have to excuse me since I just woke up, but who is this?"

"Oh, my apology, this is Barbara."

Now that I knew who it was, I had two emotions. One was I was excited to hear her voice, if you know what I mean by excited;

the other was to give her the bum's rush and tell her a pot was boiling over and I had to run and I would call her back later then wait a couple of days. But I was curious why she was calling so early, and what kind of offer was she talking about? "Go ahead, I think my head is starting to clear, what's your offer?" Down deep, I was hoping for the grand prize of a – now how can I put this in a PG phrase? Oh, let's just say I wouldn't turn down an offer of a roll in the hay, but again, my daydreaming is getting the best of me. She, Barbara, answers me in a perky little voice, never knowing my deepest desire, and says, "I can let you use our family lawyer for your request for those police files."

"I must say you and Maggie have got me into this junior detective club."

"I was talking with Maggie last night, and even though she's a kid, she has some strong feelings you can help solve this – I hate to use the word *murder*, so I'll say *tragedy*, so what do you say? Can I send him over later today?"

I say, "Sure, send him over, I may need him for my own defense attorney." We didn't say much after that, so I forgot about fixing any coffee and headed for the bathroom to shower and shave. I wanted to make myself presentable. But that plan fell apart; no sooner had I made it than the phone rang again. I thought it would be Barb telling me what time the lawyer would be over. Again I was quick to pick up the receiver, got it before the first ring stopped; this time I was cute. I answered, "Hello again." But it wasn't Barb; it was a man's voice, and he said, "I take it you're expecting a call, I'm sorry. I will be just a moment and be off the line. My name is Nick Jeffries, and I'm with the Riverside Police Department. I'm calling on behalf of Detective O'Hara, she would like to see you at one p.m. this afternoon at her office. Can I tell her you will be there?"

"I guess. I have a meeting with my lawyer today, we will see if the time schedule will work out or not. Just tell Quin I will try and make it as close to one as we can, can you do that for me, Mr. Jeffries?"

"Yes, I will give her your message. I hope you didn't miss your call. Have a nice day, good-bye." I thought, *What the hell does Quin want?* Well, I guess I would find out soon enough. With that, I was shower bound. I took extra long in the shower; it felt great, and it seemed to dilute my stress to a very tolerable level. When I did get out of the steam-encased hideaway, I felt rejuvenated. I had this gut feeling I shouldn't go with the jeans and sport shirt; my feeling was no-tennis-shoe look but a more confident, professional, may I say, debonair look. My feeling was I wanted to look like a person I wasn't; I did not want to look like the construction worker that was home watching soap operas, drinking beer, and drawing workman's compensation. I didn't know if I could pull it off or not, but I was going to give it my best shot. I went through my closet, only to find that I had one suit, one sport coat, and neckties from the seventies. It was still early morning, so I took off to do me some shopping.

I went to one of those men's warehouse stores for some everything I needed from shoes to ties. The salesman knew his stuff and fixed me up to look like a Mafia don; I mean I looked awesome. Or as Billy Crystal would say, I looked ma-va-less.

I left the store feeling pretty good about myself; I looked at my watch, and it showed almost noon. I then remembered Barb said she would send over her lawyer later today; there was no way of me knowing what time he would show up at my doorstep, and I was due at the police station in less than an hour. This was now one of the rare times I wish I carried a cell phone. My thoughts were, I would finish my appointment with Quin and get back home before the lawyer got to my place; I didn't have much choice. My stomach was starting to growl, so I needed food before my one o'clock with Quin. So as I headed toward the station, I was looking for a fast-food stop. That would prove to be little of a challenge; there seemed to be one at every corner. I chose the first one I came to and used the drive-through. Before you could say jackrabbit, I was setting the bag of hot burgers and fries next to me on the passenger seat. I pulled away from the drive-up window with one hand on the steering wheel and the other in the bag. I believe I ate my entire lunch in the space of two blocks. The large building in my direct path was that of the police department. I was somewhat of a regular, so I knew right where to park. As I got out of the car, I made a quick inventory of my pants, coat, and shoes that I didn't spill any secret sauce or any other condiments on myself.

I checked out OK, so I headed for the second floor and my mysterious call-in from the lead detective of the Hanson murder case, Quin O'Hara. As I opened the door, I took a quick peek for my friendly greeter, Officer Grandma, and there she was. I was somewhat relieved to see her there; she always put me at ease. She stood up as I entered into the room and greeted me as if I were her favorite grandson. She says to me, "Let me guess, you want to see Detective O'Hara. Am I right?" I answer with, "Wow, you must be an honest-to-goodness mind reader." I then tell her, "Yes, that's exactly who I want to see." She smiled and personally took me to Quin's desk. As we approached the desk, I could see Quin marking some sort of chart with a highlighter marker; she was deep in concentration as my guide, Officer Grandma, cut me loose and headed back in the direction of her own desk.

I found myself standing in front of her desk, not knowing if I should sit or wait for Quin's commands. I cleared my throat to break the trance Quin was evidently in. She looked up at me and gave me the blankest stare I think I have ever received. She, with a puzzled look, said, "Yes, may I help you?" I said, "You're the one who requested my attendance at one o'clock." I showed her my wristwatch, which read 12:55 p.m. "So here I am." She then turned a very bright shade of pink. "Oh, I'm so sorry, I forgot the time, plus I have to admit, I did not recognize you, Mr. Mathews. You look quite different than I have ever seen you before."

I asked, "Is that good or bad?"

"Oh, without a doubt, it's good, very good," and with that second *good*, the pink that had started to fade came blushing back. I made myself smile with that blushing-back thought. Then I thought, *Wow, this dressing up has its advantages.* "Please, sit down, I have what I think you'll consider good news. My supervisor has reconsidered your request for the police reports and the copy of the autopsy. So if you like, I can get them for you from his office, and you can take them with you today."

"I can't help but ask, why the change of heart?"

"That's because we no longer feel you are a prime suspect."

"That's great, but how did I get dropped down on the list of suspects?"

"Well, you will be reading about it in the papers tomorrow, but there has been another slaying that has all the earmarks of the same killer that murdered Audrey Hanson. We have had an eye on you the past couple of days, so we have ruled you out of this latest one, plus no one ever really thought you committed the first one."

"That's great. I feel a great weight off me. Hey, I hate to get good news and run, but I've got people coming over to my house, so I do gotta run, so if I could get those reports, I'll be on my way."

Quin says, "Yes, I can see your all dressed up and do have somewhere to go." I just smiled and let her believe whatever she wanted.

I made my way to the parking lot, not making any stops along the way, except for the quick wave gesture for Officer Grams on my way out the door. As I was about to slide into the driver's seat, I noticed the distinct aroma of French fries. That made me look down at my car seat; the smell had reminded me of my pig-like manners of eating that burger and fries on the way over to the meeting. I did not want to sit in any of my spillage and ruin my new dress slacks. The seat looked clean, but I brushed it off with the palm of my hand just in case my eyesight failed me. Being satisfied with my car seat inspection and cleaning abilities, I was headed home for my appointment with the lawyer. Due to the length of my stay with Quin, I was fortunate to have no traffic hinder my travel back home. This time, as I pulled into my driveway, I knew who belonged to the silver Corvette, plus I could see Barbara standing at my front door, talking with a man; he seemed to be about my age, with a suit that resembled mine, maybe just the slightest of shades darker. I got out of the car and made my way to the front door; the pair of Barb and her male companion held their ground and waited for me to approach them. Barb was the first to speak.

"Boy, I'm telling you, it's hard to tell which one is the lawyer, you two could open your own lawfirm, and let me tell you, I would sign up too be a client." Barb carried on. "You know, Bill, I almost didn't recognize you. I think the only reason is this is your house, and I thought I saw a car pull in your driveway, but if not for that, you got me. So how can I say this. You look great and very distinguished. I guess you can tell I'm very impressed."

The unnamed man then interrupts by saying, "I hate to break up this love fest, but I have other appointments I need to get to, so if we can take care of Mr. Mathews's needs, I will be on my way." I look at him, offer my hand, and introduce myself.

He, in an agitated voice, says, "Yes, I know who you are," and we shake hands.

I then say, "It's good you know my name, but it may benefit me somewhere down the line if I knew yours."

"Oh, I'm sorry, it's John Whitman."

"It's nice meeting you, John, please come inside where we can talk." I no sooner had unlocked the door than Barb lead us single file into the front room.

I let them go ahead and tell them, "Please make yourself at home while I get out of this coat." As I'm loosening my tie and heading for my closet, I yell out, "Can I fix anyone a drink?" The answer came back staggered but the same. "No thanks."

I hung up my coat but threw my new tie across the bed. I made my way back to the front room where my two visitors were sitting and talking. I interrupted their little chat by saying, "John, you were saying you had to run, so what can do for you, or better yet, what can you do for me?" John then explained that Barbara had told him the whole story about me being called into the police station and being refused the right to examine the files. John then told me not to worry, that he would get them for me, and that it would be no problem for him whatsoever. Also, if I would get called in again, to please give him a call, and he would accompany me the next time. With that, he stood up, reached into his inside coat pocket, and retrieved a business card and handed it to me. I thanked him, and he went over to Barbara and took her hand and said, "It was so nice seeing you again, and let's not let so many years go by between visits." She smiled and told him to call her in a couple of weeks. John seemed very pleased with that reply and shook my hand and helped himself out the front door. I never had a chance to tell either one of them that I had the reports. I stood there in the middle of the room, feeling kind of vulnerable; I don't know why. After all, it was my turf, as the young kids would say. Barbara silently taps the spot next to her on the couch; my body wants to jump, but my mind is hesitant. Like I said, Barbara is knockdown gorgeous with the body of a centerfold, but I just don't know. I know I'm out of her league, so I'm very suspect of her attention toward me.

I passed on the invitation by saying, "You're sure I can't fix you a drink? I'm having one, and no one likes to drink alone." She then said, "OK, but make it a small one." As I headed toward the kitchen, I noticed her standing up and making her way directly behind me. I turned and told her, "You don't have to get up, I'll bring it to you."

She said, "No, that's all right, I want to hear how your visit went with that cop lady."

"You mean Detective Quin," I said.

"Yes, that's right, I forget you guys are friends." I said, "I don't know about that. We know each other through the investigation of the slaying, and she was very nice with the questioning of Maggie, so yes, I think she's OK."

"Yeah, OK, you're right, she seems like an all-right sort, but tell me, how did the questioning go?"

"To tell you the truth, it went very well, she gave me both reports. I forgot to tell John, he was in such a hurry it didn't enter my mind. Maybe I would have remembered if they were in my hand, but I left them on the front seat of my car." Barbara says in a somewhat agitated voice, "Well, go get them, I'm so curious to see what they found, plus the autopsy may let me know if my sister suffered a great deal. Please go get them and fix the drinks when you come back." I didn't even answer her; I just headed for the driveway and my car. I retrieved the desired documents and headed back. As I was walking back with folders in hand, I thought to myself, *I feel like a golden retriever with a bird in his mouth, headed back to his master.*

As I opened the front door, I was met with the outstretched hand of Barbara and the request, "Can I look those over as you're fixing our drinks?" I hand them over and say, "Yeah, that will be fine." As I reach to bring down two drinking glasses from the cabinet, my mind starts thinking, *This Barbara can be a real pain in the ass. She's very demanding and somewhat of a spoiled brat. But I guess that's due to the fact she's so attractive and been pampered since birth, by not only her parents but also every school teacher and boss she's ever had in the work world.*

As I was putting the ice in the glasses, she yells out from her perch on the couch, "Bill, why did Quin decide to give you the reports?"

"Because I was dropped from the suspects' list and was no longer considered a realistic suspect, so her supervisor gave her the OK to release the reports."

"That's great news. I bet that's a weight off your shoulders."

"No kidding, I feel like I can exhale, I've been holding my breath since I was first called in."

"That's good, I'm glad you can relax a bit, but tell me, if you moved down the list of suspects, who moved up? I didn't know they had any list at all."

"Oh, I don't either. I was just told there was another murder that matched your sister's, and they knew where I was at the time this homicide took place, so I was removed as a prime suspect, get me?"

"Yeah, I get you. But come look at these reports with me. It says here in the police report the sliding glass door leading into the kitchen was not locked, and my sister was still in her nightgown, so she must have opened the door for the intruder, or Roger never locked it the night before. Also, my sister was ironing, and the crime scene showed very little struggle, so little that the stack of clothes she had already ironed were still stacked up and never knocked over even though the ironing board was. Also, it says here there was no blood found in any other room, so that tells me the whole attack took place in a small area of the kitchen. She never had a chance to run from her attacker, so the way I see it is she must have turned her back to the intruder, meaning she felt no threat." As Barbara was reading through the police report, I was reading the autopsy. I was reading each word slowly and carefully, trying to visualize the crime as it took place. As I was reading, I had to admit that I tuned out Barbara's constant chatter until it was just a hum in the background.

After reading only one sentence of the autopsy, I could already tell how vivid and descriptive it was going to be. It gave me the chills as I read it. I thought, *God, what a way to have your life end.* I just couldn't imagine anyone doing this to another human. As I read on, the hum of Barbara turned into complete silence. I was transfixed with every word; the report showed Audrey was stabbed sixteen times all in the chest area, not one near the throat, meaning to me she was being held by the throat, most likely with the forearm of the attacker. The wounds were consistent of that of a right-handed man. Also, the knife or weapon used was approximately seven to eight inches in length and very sharp; there were no jagged or torn entry or exit wounds. Four of the sixteen puncture wounds were directly into the heart; the rest were all in a cluster near or about the heart, meaning the attacker was trying for a kill throughout the entire struggle. The examiner preparing the autopsy believes the victim was dead within the first minutes of the assault. Now after reading this over, I came to the conclusion that this attacker was very lucky it didn't take longer, or this person knew how to kill fast. As my thoughts went to the possibility of more than one killer, I was socked by a fist into my bicep. "Hey, wake up, I've been talking to you. Do you want to hear my theories on my sister's murder, or are you workin' this case solo?"

"No, not at all, I was really learning quite a bit from this autopsy report. It tells you a lot about what could have happened that dreadful morning. What about you? Did you find anything useful in your police report?"

"Yeah, I think I did. The attack took place in the kitchen, and Audrey never fought back. That tells me it was a surprise attack." I was about to agree with her assumption when the phone started ringing. I set my drink down just as I was about to take my first taste. "Hello." The reply came back fast and full of excitement. "Bill, guess who?" This time I wasn't taken off guard. "Hey, Maggie, how are you?"

"Oh, I guess I'm doing OK. Is Aunt Barbara there?"

"Why yes, she is, would you like to speak with her?"

"Yeah, Grams told me she might be there."

"Hold on, I'll get her." I guess Barb overheard the conversation because when I turned to call her, she was within arm's length of the phone. "Yes, sweetie, what's up?" I could only hear Barbs' side of the conversation, and it went like this: "Yes, I will call them right now, thanks for getting hold of me, love you." There was a pause, then the words, "He's right here." With that, she hands the phone back to me.

"Hello again," I say. She then tells me she has checked with her grandmother and I'm invited to dinner this evening. I say, "That's great, I want to see you, what time is dinner?"

I hear Mags yell out, "Grams, what time is dinner? Bill wants to know." I can hear the answer in the background. "Tell him seven will be fine." Mags relays the message. "She said seven, is that going to be OK for you?"

I answer, "No problem, I'll be there." As I'm confirming my date for dinner, I'm tapped on the shoulder by Barbara, telling me she's got to go; she was called in to work. I finish off my call with Maggie and walked Barbara to her car. As she gets into her car, she says, "Let's try and go over those reports tomorrow, I'll call you when I get off work. Will that work out for you, or do you have plans set up?" I didn't, but I had enough of her for a while, so I said, "Oh, I'm sorry, but I do, but we will get together within the next couple of days, if that will work out for you?" I could see in her face she was irritated, and that gave me a warm glow inside my ego department. I think down deep, she thought she had me on a leash. I was proud to prove her wrong, at least for this day. She pulled her car door closed, started backing out the driveway, and said "Bye," leaving out the word *good*, and peeled out down the street. As I was walking back to the house, I couldn't help but think, *That girl always seems to leave in a hurry and a huff.*

By the time I had reached the front door, my thoughts of Barbara were fading, and my thoughts of my little buddy Maggie were crystallizing in my mind. I thought, *I really miss talking with her. In fact, I would much rather spend my time with Mags than her flighty aunt Barb.* I went back into my bedroom to retrieve my tie and jacket; I wanted to make a better impression on Mrs. Knowland.

If I could gain her confidence, maybe I would be able to take Mags places, like the movies, the zoo, or one of those theme parks; she needed to be a kid and get out and have fun. I didn't know for sure, but I got the impression Roger wasn't the kind of guy who would think much of his daughter's wants and needs. My assessment of Roger was Roger took care of his wants first. Maggie would just have to wait her turn for her daddy's affection and attention. I finished off redressing, ran a comb through my thinning hair, then redirected my thoughts to my drink and picked it up and put it to my lips as I had done only minutes ago; it was strong and very satisfying. I knew I had to be on my way, so after a short pause for air, I finished it off with one more swallow.

In what only seemed like a blink, I found myself ringing Mrs. Knowland's doorbell. As I stood there at the front door,

I could hear from inside the house sounds of running feet headed in my direction. The sound stopped just behind the huge, wide double doors, and then one side swung open with the smiling face of my little buddy. The greeting was a smile and a hug around my waist and a bowed head into my midsection; I thought to myself, *This is just about the best feeling a man can get.* I came right out and told her, "You know, this is the best greeting I have ever had in my life, and I mean it, cross my heart." She took a step back to look in my eyes and try and tell if I really truly meant my words. She smiled bigger than ever, knowing my words were true, then said, "Wow, Bill, you look like a movie star, I didn't know you were so handsome. Come, I want to show you to Grams." She took my hand and led me away as I used one hand to swing the door close behind us. Then the words "Grams, Grams" echoed throughout the large entryway. "Come see Bill, you won't recognize him." I thought to myself, *Was I that much of a dud that my new clothes have made that much of an impression on so many?*

Mrs. Knowland entered the room, looking quite elegant; she was wearing a white blouse with a blue skirt that came to the level of her kneecaps and wearing matching pearl earrings and necklace. She offered her hand in greeting, just as she did the first time we met. This time, however, I didn't have the urge to bend a knee and kiss her hand. "Hello, it's so nice to see you again, and thank you so much for the dinner invitation."

"Oh, you're quite welcome. As you know, our dear Maggie here," she says as she pats Mags's head, "has taken quite a liking to you." I say, "Yes, and the feeling's mutual."

"Shall we go into the dining room,?" she said, extending her arm in the direction of another room. "Yes, please show me the way." Maggie squeezes around her grandmother and comes around to me and grabs my hand to indicate she wants me to hold hers. As we enter into a very spacious dining room, I notice Roger sitting at the table, looking somewhat disheveled, with a cocktail in his hand more than halfway gone. When he notices me, he says in a somewhat slurred voice, "Hey, if it isn't my good neighbor Bill, now I won't have to drink alone, my good neighbor Bill is here." Repeating himself, he starts to stand, and that's when we both know he's wasted. He sways and then flops back down in his chair. Maggie tugs at my arm and whispers, "He's drunk." Mrs. Knowland comes right out and says, "There will be no more drinks for you, Roger, you can't even stand up, but if Mr. Mathews would like a drink, he is more than welcome." I answer quickly, "No. No thank you, but thank you for offering."

"You're quite welcome," she replies, "now please find a seat, and we will start with our salads." The dinner was great, but Roger excused himself as soon as the main course was set in front of him. Shortly after that, Maggie asked if she also could be excused; she wanted to check on her father. Mrs. Knowland nodded yes, and Maggie was off in a trot to check on her father. I waited till Maggie was out of earshot and said to Mrs. Knowland, "It's kind of difficult to distinguish which one is the parent, isn't it?"

"Yes, Roger, has not held up very well at all. Instead of him comforting his daughter, it's the other way around, as you can see. Mr. Mathews, can I tell you what I think? I want to say this quickly before she gets back, but I believe she sees you as the father figure, not Roger." I couldn't answer. Maggie came back into the room, telling us, "He's going to be fine, he went to sleep, and I covered him, so he'll sleep till the morning."

"Maggie, I must say, you are one incredible daughter."

"Thanks, Bill, but I think any child would take care of their parents if they needed it, but what I want to know is why you're all dressed up. Did you and Aunt Barbara go out somewhere?"

"No, I had a meeting in the city, and I thought it best if I were dressed up a bit. But forget about me, I want to know how you have been. I think about you every day."

"Well, to tell you the truth, I miss mom so much. I start to cry when I think about not ever seeing her again. Dad doesn't want to go back to the house, he said he wants to sell it. He tells me there are too many memories there and starts to cry. I think dad cries as much as me. Well, I can understand his reasoning, sometimes it's just better to start over new."

Mrs. Knowland enters the conversation by saying, "You and your dad can stay here as long as you like, you know there's plenty of room."

"I know, Grams, and you're the best grandmother ever." Mrs. Knowland asks if I would like dessert and maybe a cup of coffee. I say, "No thanks, I'm fine, I would just like to visit with Maggie." Then Mags realizes she's got some other stuff she wanted to show me in her room. "Hey, Bill, remember when you were here last time? I was about to show you some stuff, but you and Quin had to go."

"Yes, that's right, so you lead the way, I want to see what you got." We made our way upstairs to her bedroom. No sooner had we entered her room than she instructed me to sit down on her bed. "Now you just sit here, and I will bring the stuff to you."

I say, "That sounds good to me, bring it on." Now for the next few minutes, I see school awards for spelling, penmanship, art, and creative writing. I tell her, "Your mom and dad must have been so proud of you for these wonderful achievements." She then brings out more photos, many of Maggie's early years of life, such as her first birthday, Halloween, starting school, and some photos of her being presented the aforementioned awards. I see Mag's mom and dad, I see both Grandparents, see others in the photos, which I'm sure are friends from work or neighbors, but never any sight of Barbara. I ask, "Mags, was Aunt Barbara ever at any of your celebrations?"

"No, I don't remember ever seeing her at anything we did, even Christmas. But I do remember one time Mom and Aunt Barbara arguing, and they were mad at each other, but when my mom noticed me in the doorway, they stopped yelling, I think that was the last time she was ever over at our house."

"Gee, that's too bad, I hate to hear about brothers or sisters arguing and never making up before one of them passes away. I would think, that's a terrible thing to have to live with the rest of your life."

"Yeah, I know what you mean, but Aunt Barbara doesn't show very much emotion over anything, I don't think I have ever seen her laugh. And I know for sure I've never seen her cry. But I like her anyway. After all, she is my aunt. But let's not talk about her or my mom, I got more photos I want you to see." And with that, a stream of photos were shown to me with word commentary for each one, but one of the photos caught my eye. It was a photo of a Halloween costume Maggie was wearing; she was dressed up as a doctor, ready to do surgery. She had the head cover, the mask, the gloves, and even the foot covers for her shoes. I said, "This is quite a getup, you look like a real doctor, ready to operate."

"Yeah, I remember this Halloween because Mom didn't have to make me a costume like she always did. Grams brought all the stuff over and told Mom it might be a good outfit for Halloween. I remember mom saying yes, it would be a great costume. But then mom asked Grams if she asked Aunt Barbara if she could use it. I remember Grams telling mom, 'Oh no, this was Barbara's idea for a costume for a party at the hospital, and I asked her if she had extra for Maggie,' and she said she could get more, the stuff is dirt cheap, and handed Grams what she had. Mom said, 'Well, that was nice.' and she was really very surprised." Just as Mags was about to show me the last couple of photos, a familiar voice rang out from the stairway. "Hello, where is everybody?" Maggie enthusiastically yells out, "We're in my bedroom." A moment later, Aunt Barbara is peeking in the door.

She says, "What are you guys up to?" Maggie darts over to show Barbara the last few photos we had just looked at, including the

Halloween doctor getup. Maggie asks, "Do you remember this one, the one of me as a doctor?"

"Oh yes, I can't forget that one because we both had the same costume that year. Listen, I'm going back downstairs and getting some leftovers, I'm starved. I worked straight through my dinner hour, so I'll see you guys a bit later." Maggie speaks up,

"No, that's OK, Bill and I are done, we'll go downstairs with you." And with that, we all made our way back down. As we reached the dining room, I made the announcement I had to be on my way, but I made sure I tracked down Mrs. Knowland to thank her for a very enjoyable evening. Maggie asked, "You'll come over again, won't you, Bill?"

"Yes, I promise, next time maybe you and I can go pick out a pizza like we did before and share it with Grams and your Aunt Barbara"

"Yeah, that's a good idea." And as I started to wave good-bye to Barb, she says, "Don't forget I want to finish those reports you have, I'll call you in the morning." I say, "That will be fine, but make sure you call, I may be out, I have some things I need to take care of." Little did she know I didn't have any plans at all, I just wanted to make sure I was the one who decided when she could resume her personal investigation. After saying my farewells and a final good-bye hug for Maggie, I was headed home. On my drive, I kept thinking of that picture of Mags in the surgeon's attire, something bothered me. I don't know what, but it seemed unsettling. I was looking at something but didn't see it. After arriving home, I decided to start reading those reports again. I started with the police report; I would read this just as I did the autopsy, slowly and carefully. I didn't want to miss anything that might be insightful or imperative to solving the murder. I sat there and read it over and over, trying to get a feel for the crime as it took place. After reading it for what seemed like ten times, I came to the conclusion the attack from start to finish took no more than three minutes.

Involuntarily, my eyes started to close. I became aware that my mind and body were shutting down. I was not even going to attempt the short distance too my bed; I just lay down in place and was out.

The morning arrived with me still clutching the reports in one hand; I got up, my head swirling with thoughts of all I had reviewed the night before. I thought I wanted to talk with Quin. I had some very interesting theories on this case, some she had to take seriously, and some questions that I was very anxious to hear her explain. I was now pumped up, and my adrenalin flowing, I looked for her business card and gave her a call. She answered. I didn't waste any time with small talk I got right to the meat of the call and almost pleaded for an audience with her ASAP. She said I could come in and see her but to make it quick; she was leaving in less than two hours. I told myself, *No time for showers, coffee, or shave.* I exchanged my suit pants and dress shoes and shirt for jeans, sweatshirt, and tennis shoes.(Aw, to feel like me again.) In no time, I was standing at the desk of Detective Quin; she told me right off, "Now that's the Bill Mathews I recognize."

This time, I was the one blushing. "OK, I get it, I'm the guy everyone recognizes as a slob."

"No, no, I wouldn't say that, I would say you dress very casual."

"OK, casual or formal, I'm here to discuss the Hanson murder, and my time is limited, so can I start asking you a few questions?"

"Yes, go ahead. I'm sorry for my unprofessional manners."

"No, that's all right, here is my first question. What do you know about Barbara Knowland and a lawyer named John Whitman?"

"We know Barbara is the sister of the deceased, Audrey Hanson. As far as Mr. Whitman, I never heard of him, but let me run his name and see what comes up." She then picks up her phone and tells someone on the other end, "Give me a profile on a Mr. John Whitman, a practicing lawyer in the area." She then turns to me and says, "That will only take a couple of minutes, and we will get a printout on his professional history. What else do you have for me as we wait?"

"Yeah, have you completely ruled out Roger having any part in his wife's murder?"

"I would say at this time, yes, we don't believe he had any part. Why do you ask?"

"I went over to the Knowland's for dinner last night, and Roger was pretty well lit, and to me, it's hard to tell if he's drinking because of sorrow or guilt. Anyway, it's just a thought." Before she can give me a thought on that, a young man comes up behind her and sets some papers down on her desk. She picks them up and starts to look them over; she's very intense with her survey of the information within. Her silence is broken with a one-word comment: "Interesting." She's got me on the edge of my chair with curiosity. "You're killing me here, what did you find?"

"Well, it seems Mr. Whitman defended Ms. Knowland in a harassment suit a few years back."

"Let me guess, she harassed her boss somewhere because he didn't pay enough attention to her?"

"No, it wasn't quite like that at all. In fact, it's somewhat unusual."

"How so?"

"It shows here she was harassing her supervisor's wife. She was a nurse's aide, and I guess she had a fling with one of the doctors, and his wife found out and confronted Ms. Knowland, but it seems the confrontation backfired. Because it says here that Ms. Knowland told the wife to leave them alone, that this doctor wanted to be with her and her alone. But that was not the case. The doctor wanted to save his marriage and told Barbara to take a hike, but I guess she just couldn't believe that was true and blamed the wife, therefore the constant harassment. It went to court, where she was given a suspended sentence and ordered to complete an anger management class."

"Well, I'm wondering if that anger management class did any good. And just a thought, this new murder you told me about, was a female involved?"

"Why yes, it did," answered Quin, "and get this, the victim was the wife of a doctor."

"Wow, I can't think of another word to describe how I feel." Quin quickly threw a wet towel on my enthusiasm. "Just slow down there, Bill, for all we know, Ms. Knowland has an airtight alibi."

"Well, that might prove to be true, but my guess is she won't, and that brings me to another question. The fibers you found at the crime scene, would they happen to be consistent with the fibers you find in a surgical mask and head cover and those little booties doctors wear?"

"That I couldn't tell you, but I can give the evidence department a call and check with them."

"Yes, I would appreciate if you did that, and believe me, I'll bet you a dime to a doughnut the results will come back as a match."

"I'm sorry, I will have to pass on that wager, plus you will have to wait to find out if you would have won or lost. I have an appointment, so I won't know the results until I get back later this afternoon."

"Oh, I'm sorry, you told me that this morning. I just got rolling and I forgot all about your appointment."

"That's OK, I'll give you a call later today and let you know what I found out from the lab."

"Thanks, I really would appreciate that." I shook her hand and was out of there. I needed to talk with Mrs. Knowland ASAP, and my suspicions were all falling into place. But I had one big question that needed to be answered, and the matriarch of the family may have the answer I needed. I wasn't going to be presumptuous and drive over there and ring the doorbell; no, I would phone and ask for permission for a private audience. She was old school, and I wanted to play by her rules. I do think she took a liking to me; I was polite, and Maggie really liked me, so that had to be good for a few brownie points. I went back home for a bite to eat and change of clothes; no tie, but sport coat and slacks would fit the bill. I made the call over to the Knowland place and got Mags answering the phone; she was her joyous and cheerful self when she recognized my voice, and that always made my heart melt with joy.

I said, "Hi, kid, I need to speak with your grandma."

She said "Sure." I could hear her yell out in her own fashion for Grams. Mags told me she's on her way and then tells me "Grams hates when I yell out for her, she tells me it's not ladylike. But here she is, Bill, I'll talk with you later. Bye."

"Hello, Mr. Mathews, what can I do for you?"

"Hello, Mrs. Knowland, I'm sorry to bother you, but I would like to know if it would be possible if I came by in the next hour or so and ask you some questions?"

"May I ask pertaining to what?"

"It has to do with your daughters' relationship with each other."

"Mr. Mathews, could you be a little more specific!"

"I would rather not discuss this over the phone, that's why I wanted to come by and talk with you in person."

"Very well, come by and we will talk."

"Thank you very much. I will head over that way immediately." On my way over, my mind played out all the possible ways I could open the topic of how her youngest daughter might have had some involvement with her eldest daughter's death. As I drove, my stomach started to twist and turn I thought, *Who am I to tell a mother that one daughter might have killed the other?* Was I, as Quin said, jumping the gun? I should have waited until the forensic results came back and if Barbara indeed had an airtight alibi. I was beginning to think I should call this meeting off; I may have put the proverbial cart before the horse.

But I had a thought; I could give Quin a call and see if the lab got the results back. That might give me more ammunition to plead my case that daughter number 2 had a hand in the slaying of daughter number 1. Or I could just go with what I had and let Mrs. Knowland tell me what she thinks it all adds up to. I was almost to the house and I decided I will just tell Mrs. K all that I knew and all I suspected and let the chips fall where they may. I was there for one reason; that was to find out if Barbara had a hatred for her sister that was so deep she wanted her dead.

I hoped I would find out the answer to that question within the next few minutes because I was now pulling into the very long driveway of the Knowland house and knowing only moments later, I would be at the front door, which I considered the point of no return. If I was to bail out, it was now. As I had now come to a complete stop, I just sat there, going over what I would say or how I should say it. Again, my insides were turning, and again, I felt queasy talking too myself out loud. "You're a fool, drive away." And just as my quivering fingers started to turn the ignition key, I could hear tapping on my driver side window. I must have been in a subconscious trance; I turned and saw the smiling face of my little buddy Maggie. She said, "Hey, are you coming in or not?" I smiled back at her and then let myself out of the car. We reached for each other's hand and made our way to the house. "Hello," came from the front porch near the giant double doors that led into the house. It was Mrs. Knowland, and as always, she looked – as the British would say – smashing, this lady. And I don't use that word very often to describe an older woman, but she fit the word perfectly. She indeed was a Lady.

With our hands intertwined, Maggie and I headed up the front steps; before reaching the porch, I gave out my response to Mrs. Knowland's hello with something original. "Good afternoon, Mrs. Knowland." She said, "Please come in," as she held one of the double doors open for my entrance. "We'll talk in the study, Mr. Mathews." I thought, *This might be the only time in my life*. Other than a movie, I heard the term *study* used to describe a room in a house. But sure enough, she led me into a room with a large oak desk and walls with shelves filled with books. The only thing missing was the large leather chair; in its place was a plaid-covered lazy-boy recliner. And small love seat-type couches. Mrs. K instructs me to please be seated. I chose the love seat, leaving her the desk chair or the recliner; she took the chair behind the desk, and this arrangement left me feeling like I was in the principal's office.

Once seated, I got right into it but was careful not to come on too strong. I asked, "How did your daughters get along growing up?" Mrs. K. immediately leaned back in her chair then seemed to drift back into time; she just sat there for what seemed like minutes. Then like being snapped out of a hypnotic state, she apologizes, "Oh, I'm so sorry, Mr. Mathews, I just got caught up in some very pleasant memories. I think your question about the girls triggered a flashback when the girls were six and eight or five and seven, they were so close they had so much fun doing things together. And it stayed that way all the way up to the high school years."

"Well, I have to ask, what changed between them during the high school years?" This time, Mrs. Knowland did just the opposite from the first question; this time she brought her chair up to the edge of the desk and proceeded to put her elbow on the desk and her hand under her chin, striking the thinker pose. "You know, Mr. Mathews, your questions are bringing me full circle with my emotions.

"As I said, the girls got along great as youngsters, but as teenagers, it was a much different story. Both Audrey and Barbara were very good students. Audrey was involved with school plays and the student newspaper, while Barbara ran track and was a cheerleader in the fall. It all went along very smoothly until I believe it was Barb's sophomore year. Yes, I remember because Audrey was a senior, and that whole senior dance thing happened."

I interrupted. "I'm sorry, what dance thing happened?"

"Oh, what a mess that was, I think it was right then and there they started to drift apart as sisters.

"If I were to blame anyone, it would be that boy. Oh, how I disliked that boy, I will never forget his name, Lester Aster, Aster as in disaster, because that's what he caused in our household. This Lester boy had asked Barbara to the senior dance well, in advance of the event, and Barbara being, an underclassman, was thrilled that a senior had asked her. I was told by both girls that underclass students are rarely asked to that particular dance, it was quite a compliment. But the problem occurred just a week before the dance. That little SOB – excuse my language, Mr. Mathews – canceled the date with Barbara and told her he invited a senior who had not been asked and thought she would understand. That senior was Audrey, and Audrey never knew it was Lester who had invited Barbara. If she had, she would never had accepted.

This was a complete, as I said, disaster. I remember being very upset and asking Barbara why she didn't tell Audrey the name of the boy who asked her to the dance, and she had a very good and sincere answer. I remember her telling me through sobbing tears, 'Mom, I didn't want to make a big deal about it, I actually wanted to downplay it because I knew "Aud" had not been asked, and she is a senior.' I knew how sad she must have felt, and I didn't want to carry on, so I said as little as possible. Now do you understand? I felt so ashamed for being cross with her. I went over and gave her a hug and told her I was sorry for acting the way I did. She hugged me back, and I began to weep."

"I remember at the time things seemed to settle down. Audrey ended up telling that boy she did not want to go to the dance due to the circumstances she was invited, so neither girl went. The rest of the school year went along uneventful. Audrey graduated, and Barbara became a junior that summer, and that's when things started to change. Barb got a job as a lifeguard at the community pool, Audrey went to visit some of the colleges where she may enroll."

"Mrs. Knowland, in what way did things start to change?"

"It was small things at first, but they were so out of place for Barbara's personality. First, she started showing up late for her job at the pool, then a run-in with some of the girls that were regulars every summer at the pool. It was so far out of her character I had to talk with her. She said it was no big deal, that she was late only a couple of times, and it was only a minute or two she was late. And as far as the girls, she said they were talking about her, and she called them out on it, and they were all a bunch of – excuse the term – bitches. I never in my life ever heard either daughter use such language. I knew then, something was going on with my baby. I talked it over with Mr. Knowland, he was living here back then. I wanted Barb to see a doctor, see if she had some hidden anger that we didn't know about, something she could share with a professional person, and, if needed, some sort of medication."

"Well, tell me, how did the doctor experiment work out? Or did she even agree to go?"

"Oh yes, she went, in fact, she went for almost a year, but the strangest thing happened. After," she paused, "I would say ten or eleven months, the doctor calls us and tells us Barb should start seeing a different doctor. We ask why, was there a problem? He tells my husband and me it's a patient-doctor privilege and he cannot discuss it any further with us."

"Did you find a new doctor for her?"

"No, we never did, but it wasn't due to lack of trying, she tried maybe four or five. She hated them all, we just gave up, she refused to see anyone."

"So then what happened? Did she show improvement, how was her behavior? Better, worse, the same?"

"Mr. Mathews, I have no idea why I'm telling you all this, but if you think it will help in any way, then I will continue."

"Yes, I think it will help, there are several unanswered questions concerning the death of your eldest daughter."

"Wait, wait, you hold it right there, mister. Are you telling me you think Barbara had something to do with her sister's death? Are you insane? They were sisters. Sisters don't kill each other, why in the world would you even think something like that?"

"I'm terribly sorry for upsetting you, Mrs. Knowland. It's just so many things add up to Barbara's involvement." Mrs. Knowland now stands in defiance, both hands clinched in a fist and resting on the desktop. "And just exactly what things are you talking about?" *Her sudden mood swing caught me off guard.* I just sat there, looking down at my feet, and remained speechless. She spoke again, even with a firmer voice. "I'm waiting, Mr. Mathews, what things are you speaking of?" I had to play my cards now; I couldn't hold back. I had to tell her everything we knew and everything I suspected. I started by asking her to "Please sit back down, and I will tell you what I know." She obliged me and sat back down. I then started by telling her about the stalking and the arrest, the latest murder of a doctor's wife, a wife that belonged to a doctor the police believe Barbara was having an affair with, just as was the case of the stalking crime.

"The reason I came over here was to ask you, do you know of any reason Barbara would be so angry with her sister she would want to harm her? The reason I ask is evidence from both homicides match *here is where I was taking a chance the forensic evidence would match from both scenes* – small fibers consistent with doctors' surgical mask, head cover, and those little booties that go over shoes. Barbara has access to all kinds of that stuff, doesn't she?"

"Why yes, I suppose she does."

"And the day of the attack on Audrey." I didn't want to use the word *murder* just yet, so I continued, "The police and I believe Audrey knew her attacker and felt no threat and opened the sliding glass doors and let them in, only to turn her back to them so she could return to ironing and was grabbed from behind by the neck and, well, you know from there. So again, do you know of any motive Barbara would have had?"

"Mr. Mathews, I was telling you about Barbara and the trouble she had finding a second psychiatric doctor. As it turned out, she was coming on to the male doctors and refused to be seen by a female. Her outbursts and temper tantrums became more violent and more frequent, and she was hospitalized her entire high school senior year. She seemed to get well through counseling and medication, but here is what I think you came to hear. When Barbara was released, she found a job as a file clerk with an insurance company. Things went very well for several months until a young executive started paying attention to her and eventually asked her out. Barbara was very happy and by all accounts seemed well structured. But her happiness was short-lived. The young man she fell for found someone else and asked the new one to marry him. His new love was none other than Audrey, Barbara's sister. Roger went from lover to brother-in-law. Barbara showed no anger or jealousy whatsoever. She said she was happy for the both of them, even going as far as telling Roger, Audrey was better suited for him and telling Audrey she liked Roger a lot but was never in love with him. It all sounded like the truth, Barb convinced us all."

"Evidently, she was more upset then she let on."

"Bill, I just don't understand why she showed no anger or hostility for so many years."

"Well, Mrs. Knowland *noticing that she called me by my first name*, that I couldn't possibly answer, that would take someone with experience in this type of matter."

"You know Barbara showed so much care and affection during "Aud's" pregnancy, I would never have thought she carried such animosity."

"Mrs. Knowland, I can't say for sure, but I would think someone with a very delicate psyche could have a rage buried deep within, just waiting for something to trigger it."

"Please call me Ruth. I think we have come to the point we can refer to each other by first names."

"Thank you, I feel likewise."

"Tell me, Bill, do the police feel Barbara is responsible for Audrey's death?"

"That I can't answer, all I can tell you is they will be calling her in for questioning. And if you would please excuse me, I need to make a call, *the day I went out and got the new suit and such, I also went the whole nine yards and invested in a cell phone, and as it turned out I needed it now. I kept in my car and I was about to use it for the first time* I told Ruth I will be right back, and I may have more information on the case." I made my way out to the car, called Quin direct, and found out the fibers matched at both crime scenes and Barbara was not at work during the window of opportunity to commit the slayings. Therefore the police had a warrant out for her arrest and were headed to the hospital as we spoke. I headed back to share my newfound information with Mrs. Know – ah, I mean Ruth.

As I reentered the room, I found her directly in the doorway. She said, "Bill, we have been talking for quite a while. What do you say about some sandwiches and something to drink?"

"Gee, that's very thoughtful Mrs. – oops, I mean Ruth." With that, she slowly walked away in the direction of the kitchen. I stuck my head back out the door, looking for Maggie. I found no sight or sound of the little one. I walked back into the room and as I waited for Ruth's return I started to look through the books that covered three of the four walls of the room; I thought, *They must be for show. No one really reads this kind of bullshit.* Architecture of Early Rome, The True Meaning of the Great Wall of China.

My daydreaming was broken by Ruth asking me if I had seen Maggie. I said, "No, but it's funny you should ask because I just took a look for her myself." At that precise time, the Knowland house phone rang; only steps away from Ruth, she picked it up. I could only hear this side of the conversation. "Hello. Yes, it is. No,

I haven't seen her since dinner last night. Let me check." Holding one hand over the receiver, Ruth asks me to check outside and see if Barbara's car is out front; I check quickly and come back with the reply, "No sign of her car." She proceeded, "No, her car is not here. Very well, come right over, we will be here." She then hangs up and gives me this puzzled look. "It seems Barbara was confronted at work by the police, and she skipped out when they let her go to change her clothes. But right now, I'm concerned about Maggie, she never strays. Let me check again outside." Ruth went out to the backyard, it's a very wide and deep yard covered with lush green grass and surrounded by beautiful shade trees. There was a brick patio right out the steps from the house, and beyond that, thirty feet or so, was a swimming pool and next to the pool were reclining lounge chairs, all vacant but one. And in that occupied chair was a man, I would say, two in half sheets to the wind. Ruth approached him and said in tones I had never heard from Ruth before, "Roger, snap out of it, have you seen Maggie?" With his hand covering his eyes from the glare, he slurred the words, "Hey, don't panic, Ma. She went with Barbara somewhere."

"Where did they go?"

"Hell if I know, what's all the fuss?"

"Never mind, just go on doing what you're doing – nothing. You're real good at that." And with that, we both headed back to the house to wait for the police.

As we made our way back to the library, Ruth just shook her head in the "no" fashion and muttered, "Roger has become a lost cause, he is absolutely worthless as a father." Then she stops in her tracks and turns toward me and says, "I'm so sorry, Bill, here I am mumbling to myself, and I still haven't gotten you any lunch. You go sit down, and I will bring you in something."

I tell her, "Don't worry about me, I'm fine."

"Don't be silly. It's all been prepared!" So I did as instructed; I went and sat in the library. In moments, Ruth was bringing in a tray with sandwiches, chips, and a cold soda with a glass full of ice standing next to it. I jump up and take the tray from her, at the same time asking, "What about you? Aren't you having anything?"

"No, I have lost my appetite. I'm worried sick about my little Maggie. Why in the world would Barbara come home to get Maggie? Especially, if she's trying to elude the police."

"I have no idea what goes through your daughter's mind, but when the police get here, we may get more answers."

As we sat in that room, it seemed to me that the room itself knew of the grief that was being felt; it was as if the library became larger just so it could contain the expanding sorrow as it reached its crescendo.

Breaking the silence was Ruth; I believe she was talking too herself, but loudly enough so I could hear her. She said, "I wonder if it was something I did or said, or maybe it was something I should have said. Was I too strict, or too lenient?" I had to interrupt. "Ruth, stop beating yourself up. Sometimes things like this just happen." As I was about to tell her about the mental illness described as bipolar disorder, the doorbell started its musical chimes. Ruth let out a sigh as she got up to answer the door. "Oh, how I hope they have found the girls and they're safe." As she opened the huge double doors, there greeting her were Homicide Detective Quin O'Hara and a somewhat weathered middle-aged uniformed police officer. Quin reintroduced herself to Mrs. Knowland, not knowing if she would remember her from the luncheon that was held after Audrey's funeral, then nodded toward the uniformed officer and said, "This is Sergeant Roye, and with your permission, he would like to look through the house.

"Please, help yourself." Quin then asked if we could find a place to talk, so back into the library we traveled. Ruth went back to her desk location. I went and pushed the recliner closer to the desk for Quin to use and I, in return went back to my little love seat. Quin then addressed Mrs. Knowland. "I'm sorry to inform you, we have an eyewitness confirming your daughter leaving the scene of a recent homicide. She was seen throwing gloves and other apparel into the backseat of her silver Corvette. We have a warrant for her arrest. As you know, when we went to serve it – she took off. We believe she came here and picked up your granddaughter, for what purpose, we do not know. Tell me, would you know of any reason?"

"None whatsoever." Just then, Sergeant Roye peeks in and exclaims, "The house is clear, I'm going to check the grounds." He turns and leaves before Quin can give a response. Just as the Sarge goes off, Quin's cell phone goes off. Ruth and I get to hear the one-sided conversation and wait to see if it will give any answers for the safety or whereabouts of Maggie. We can hear Quin's instructions. "Send three or four unmarked cars, absolutely no black and whites, I don't want her spooked. Block all street exits, and have someone keep an eye on the backyard. Bring in the negotiation team ASAP. Do you understand all my instructions? OK, get on with it. I'm heading over there now."

Quin stands and says, "I guess you heard part of that conversation. Your daughter and granddaughter have been located at Maggie's house. There will be no way for them to leave the premises. I am going over there now, and hopefully, we can negotiate a peaceful and happy ending."

"Well, Detective, Bill and I are going to be right behind you. I might be able to help in some way."

"Mrs. Knowland, that's up to you if you want to be there, but I must warn you, you will have to stay back."

"Yes, I understand, thank you, I will see you over there shortly. I think I should call Barbara's father. He should know of the severity that his youngest is in. I think it would be better that he hears it from me rather than the possibility of seeing it on television." Quin took off, and Ruth made her call. Her voice quivered as she asked to speak to Mr. Knowland. She told the person on the other end in a very indignant tone, "Tell him it's his wife."

Mr. Knowland must have been standing right next to the phone because immediately, Ruth started talking. "What are you doing, screening your calls? Just forget it, now keep your mouth shut and let me talk. The police have a warrant out for Barbara's arrest, they believe she killed a doctor's wife and is also responsible for Audrey's death. I wanted you to know firsthand rather than see it on tonight's news. I am leaving now. Maggie and Barbara are over at Audrey's house right now, and the police have it surrounded, good-bye."

Due to the volume of Mr. Knowland's voice, I could hear him yell out, "Wait a minute!" Ruth brought the phone closer to her ear. "What!"

"I want to go."

"OK, but make it quick, Mr. Knowland still in a loud voice says," Listen to me, I may be able to help the police by talking too Barb." With that, Ruth started to listen; she slumped into a chair that was next to the phone table. She just sat there. This was not a two-way conversation. Ruth never even nodded her head with the recognition of an affirmative or a negative response. In what seemed like several minutes but in actuality was only a few, Ruth hung up the phone and said, "Let's go." I asked if she was all right, and she said she would tell me on the way. And true to her word, she started to unravel a story that she herself just found out.

Ruth tells me her ex paid a little extra to the first doctor, a.k.a. psychiatrist and psychoanalyst, to keep him up-to-date on the severity of his daughter's mental health. The doctor told Mr. Knowland, who has a first name of Phillip. I had to ask Ruth; I tired of always referring to him as Mr. Knowland. Barbara had all the signs of being psychosexual, psychotic, and psychopathic. In short, she was one screwed-up teenager. Phillip then told Ruth that Barbara had fun flirting with the young doctor, and after several months of visits and counseling, she finally threw herself on him and tried to arouse him through all ways in her sexual arsenal, which, by the way, were many. The doctor threw her off him and explained this was not acceptable; she just laughed and said, "I know you want me, all the boys at school were coming on themselves to get next to me. You're no different, admit it." The doctor had held this back from the very first visit but had to tell her, "Barbara, I'm not interested in you. I'm gay." The doctor told him she stepped back and, with eyes of disbelief, said, "No, no, I don't believe you." It was then the doctor pulled out a photo from his wallet; it showed the doctor and a young man standing in front of a large fountain,

holding hands. She looked at that photo and said, "I am going to kill that little bastard, he's trying to convince you that you're queer so we can't be together. You'll see, I'll kill him." That's when he dropped Barb as a patient and relayed her possible homicidal tendencies.

As I was listening to Ruth relay the story she got from Phil, I thought, *Is Maggie in danger from this psycho?* We were stopped by a uniformed cop standing in front of a barricade. "Sorry, you will have to turn around, streets are closed due to police activity." I tell the cop, "Hey, Detective O'Hara is expecting us. This is the grandmother of the hostage." He tells us "Hold on" then proceeds to use his walkie-talkie to get clearance for us. You can hear the static-filled reply, "Let them through." As we weave our way around the police cars and news vans, we reach my cul-de-sac. This time, instead of wooden barricades blocking off the street, it's just yellow crime tape. No sign of uniformed police or black and white units, only unmarked cars that stand out like a sore thumb as police vehicles. Some young guy holds up the tape and motions us through. I pull the car over toward the curb but stop well short of it. I unfasten my seat belt, look over to Ruth, and say, "Hang in there, it's all going to work out." Before I can get out of the car, Quin is holding the door to keep me from extricating myself. "Please, if you will, I would very much appreciate if you both would stay in the car."

"OK, but what's taken place so far? Have you been able to communicate with either of them? Are they all right?"

"Whoa, slow down, all I can tell you right now is they are both in the house and both seem fine. They know the house is surrounded, and at this time, no one has answered our attempted phone calls. Ah, but Mr. Mathews, there is one thing I would like to ask you, and if you say no, I would completely understand.

"Well, go ahead and ask, what is it, Quin?" She somewhat sheepishly asks, "Would you let us use your house as our command post?"

"Sure, go ahead, and then maybe you will let Mrs. Knowland and myself out of the car?"

"Yes, I'm sorry, you go ahead and unlock your house for us. And I want to talk with you both about some new information on Barbara's recent behavior." The three of us headed up the short distance to my place. I unlocked the front door and turned on some lights; soon it would be getting dark. I headed out to the garage and grabbed as many bottled waters as I could carry. From there I put on a fresh pot of coffee; no telling how long we would be holed up in the command post, better known as my place. After pushing several things aside for the waters, I wanted the latest on Barb. I wasn't going to wait for Quin to bring it back up, so I just said, "Hey, what's the new info you got on Barb?"

"Oh yes. It doesn't bide well for Barbara's state of mind.

In fact, she is becoming more delusional every day.

"We brought in Dr. Baxter for questioning, he was the latest doctor Barbara was interested in, we wanted to know how long the affair had been going on with him and Barbara and when his wife found out about it. Now get this, the doctor tells us that Barbara indeed made a play for him, but he rebuffed her. She told him she knew he wanted her, but he was afraid of his wife and didn't have the balls to get rid of her. So she told the doctor, "Hold tight, babe, I'll take care of her, then we can be together." Dr. Baxter told us, he never, in his wildest imagination, thought she meant *kill*. 'I thought she was just joking around, playing off the rejection as a defense mechanism.' She showed no emotion, it was just as matter-of-factly as someone would say, "Yeah, I'll go over and take your dogs for a walk." I'm telling you, she's a nutcase and needs to be locked up.'"

Ruth starts to ask Quin a question when Quin says, "Excuse me, I have the negotiator team ready to call the house." She gets up and heads toward the kitchen; one of my two house phones is located there. As the negotiator starts to key in the number, Quin yells out, "No talking, I want quiet." The phone is hooked up to a speaker so everyone can hear the other end of the line. The phone starts to ring, then silence, then the start of a second ring, then the quiet again, only this time, before the start of the third ring, the receiver is picked up. No answer, no breathing, no background noise; the only thing that can be heard are the gears turning the reels that are on the tape recorder, the ones hooked up to the phones. The deathly calm was finally broken by these words: "Well, say something, you're the one who called me, just what the F do you want?" Only using the one letter to make her point.

"Hello, Barbara, this is Barbara?"

"Yes, and you're really starting to piss me off. You're the asshole that made the call, who else did you expect at this number? You got God knows how many people out front, you got a hundred pairs of eyes on the place, you know it's Mags and me, you know every move we make, and you ask me if this is Barbara. You are too fuckin' stupid, I got nothing to say." She hangs up. After I hear that I can't keep my mouth shut, I say, well....

"I guess I speak for most of us here when I say that went –" I pause shortly.

"Not well at all." Ruth then puts her hand on my shoulder and says, "Stay calm, Bill, they are trying their best." Quin then adds to Ruth's comments by saying, "I know it's your house, so I really don't want to ask you to leave."

I say, "I'm sorry, I'm just worried about Maggie, and no one triggers a homicidal rage out of Barbara." There is a short discussion, and all agree to give the second negotiator a try with Barbara. The phone is redialed, and Barb answers on the first ring; and everyone nods in agreement that that's is a good sign.

"Hello, Barbara, this Dave, sorry we upset you on that last call."

"Just wait a minute, Mr. Dave, don't start off being as stupid as that other jerk. What are you, fuckin' Siamese twins? Why do you start off with 'sorry we,' who in the fuck is *we*?"

"You're right, I shouldn't have said *we*, let's start over. What can I do to get you and your niece out of the house and talk with me? Not the police or lawyers or doctors, just me."

"Well, isn't that so sweet of you, but I got some questions for you, Mr. Dave."

"Go ahead, ask me anything you want, and I will try and answer the best I can."

"First, I guess all you guys out there think I'm pretty fuckin' stupid, don't you?"

"No, not at all, why would you even think such a thing?"

"Because when I turned away, and I admit I don't know how you did it, you made the ole switcheroo. You took my sweet little niece and left me with one of Roger's little tramps." Instantly, the negotiator, Quin, and everyone in the room looked at one another, and all color ran from their faces. Ruth jumped up, thinking her granddaughter was safe somewhere outside. I had to quickly dampen her enthusiasm by explaining there had been no switch; Barbara was becoming more delusional under the stress of being trapped. Ruth was slowly becoming hysterical; we had to get her out of the house. The best place would be her own home; maybe one of the plainclothes officers could take her, and possibly, Roger could sober up enough to watch over her. I myself made the call. No answer, only the answering machine. I showed Ruth to my bedroom and told her to try and lie down. She agreed and reached deep into her purse and came up with a small prescription bottle; she shook out two tablets and asked for a drink of water. As I went back into the kitchen to retrieve one of those bottled waters, I could hear Ruth still talking as I was still in the room.

"You know I usually just take one, but I think I need two pills today, what do you think, Mr. Mathews?" It was easy to see she was coming unraveled.

I said, "Yes, Mrs. Knowland, I think two would be just the right amount." She popped the pills then took my hand so I could guide her slowly down on the bed. She readjusted one of the pillows under her head then looked up at me and said, "Pray for Maggie, will you, Bill? Will you do that for me?"

I said, "Yes, I promise," and with that, she closed her eyes. I quietly left the room and closed the door behind me. I went back in the kitchen and whispered to Quin, "Where do we stand with Barbara? Is she still on the line?"

"Yes, she's on the line, but she's rambling on about Roger and why he isn't here with her. She's telling Dave, she did everything that Roger ever wanted her to do and he just shit on her. She's saying, way back when she was a little girl, her father loved her the most, but when her mother realized it,

she drove him out and divorced. She says all the men she has ever loved have been weak and been dominated by evil women." She's telling the negotiator

"At one time, I was going to kill my mother, but then I thought I will get even with her when her precious firstborn is dead, then dad will still hate her and love me all alone, I will be all he has. But where is Roger? After I killed his fucking wife for him, he would never accept my phone calls. He avoided me every time I would track him down at his restaurants, the golf course. I even went to his barbershop. He always had some lame excuse why he couldn't be with me. Now I think I know why. I scared off some of his other little whores, but I guess this one here in the house is his favorite. Dave, are you listening to me?"

"Oh yes, I'm right here but Barbara, listen, I got an idea. If you think that girl is one of Roger's favorites, why don't you take her out, kill her right in front of Roger's eyes? Just let him suffer like he has made you suffer. It would teach him a lesson and also show him who's boss. What do you think?" Dave holds his hand over the phone and mouths, "We have to act now, send in SWAT, plainclothes, FBI, I don't care who, but I believe we only have minutes before she starts slicing up that kid."

"Dave, Dave, Dave, you really have a good idea there, but you're thinking as a cop, stuff like that never works. You see, when you get two people that think they love each other, one of them will try and become heroic. That's bad. I say kill the little bitch now and let Roger see the results and sob. He will be talking to his self and sayin 'Oh my god, if I was only there, I may have been able to stop it.' You see my thinking, Dave?"

"Yes, I do, your way seems to make much more sense."

"OK. Then I'm going to go kill her now. And by the way, have all the guys with binoculars keep an eye on the front bedroom. I will open the curtains so they can see a master at work." The phone went quiet. Dave started yelling, "GO, GO, GO" We all ran to my front window and watched as twenty or more heavily armored men stormed the house. We could hear the cluster grenade go off. We could hear yelling; one very clear voice yelled, "I got her!" We had no idea who the *her* was. Then there was only a couple of male voices screaming out the command, "Let her go," repeating again, "Let her go." Then the sound of rapid gunfire, then the voice, "Grab her. See if she's still alive." The tape recorder was still turning but recording only silence, then the words we so dreaded to hear. "Sorry, sir. They're both dead."

Everyone in the room seemed to emotionally sink in unison. We all headed out the door and made our way to the Hanson house. Not one word was spoken on the way. We could hear sirens off in the distance. I thought, *Why bother, they won't be needed.* As we crossed over the street and approached the mayhem, my heart fell even further as I looked at the house. I couldn't help but think of the night my little buddy sidetracked the cop so I could go investigate, or how she wanted to see the blue ribbon for my hot-chocolate making. I just couldn't keep the tears from rolling down my cheeks. Quin saw me and came over and told me how sorry she was for me. She came right out and said she knew how much I cared for that little girl. With that pat on the back, she walked away. I thought, *Shit, I got to go back to my place and tell Ruth she has lost her other daughter and her only grandchild.*

With my head down, I turned and headed back up the street. My feet felt as heavy as my heart; I could only shuffle. I had only gone a couple of yards when I heard the loud voice yell out, "Bill!" I turned and saw Quin waving me to come back. Quin was standing at the backdoor of one of those unmarked police cars. I took only one step and she yells out again, "Damn it, hurry up." I can see it's very important; she wants my ass over there now, so heavy feet or not, I try my best to jog to her location. As I reach the car, Quin steps back and tells me, "Have a look." I put one hand on the top of the car for balance then peek my head into the backseat. I'm glad I was balancing myself because my knees buckled. There, looking me right straight in the eyes, was my little and best buddy of all time, Maggie. I dropped to my knees, reached into the car, and gave her a hug – not just a regular hug, but one for the ages. To this day, I couldn't tell you who hugged the hardest or who hugged the longest, so I will just call it a tie. I don't remember too much of what happened after that; I do remember carrying Mags back to my place and waking up Ruth with Maggie still in my arms. As far as the SWAT team and the yelling and the gunfire and that part about they're both dead, well, that took weeks to figure out what happened. But I guess I can tell it the way it was explained to me.

Roger must have come into the house from the swimming pool area when he realized Maggie might be in danger from Barbara. He knew Barbara was sometime goofy but never paid any attention to her wild notion that they could be together again now that Audrey's gone. But when Roger sensed Ruth was truly concerned about Maggie's well-being, he went to talk with her. That's where the police believe he overheard that Maggie and Barbara were at the house; he also probably heard the urgency the police were being dispatched. He knew the house they were referring to had to be his. He went straight over there, snuck in somehow, and waited and listened. I'm sure he didn't have intentions when he went over there to kill his sister-in-law, but I think in his mind, he could rescue his daughter at any time. The police think he was hidden in the bedroom closet and could hear all that was being said; he could hear a complete confession. But when Barbara said, "I'm going to kill the little bitch now" and came straight into the room with the knife and grabbed little Maggie, Roger jumped out and started strangling Barbara with one of his neckties; after all, it was his closet. But once Maggie slipped away, Roger was too full of anger and adrenalin; he had the person that killed his wife and also was about to kill his daughter. No police command was going to stop his mission, plus I doubt he ever heard the command to stop.

If you care, I'm back to work. I see Mags every weekend and if I get dressed up in my suit, I'm going to ask Detective Quin out on a date. I think Maggie and I will take her out for pizza and root beer. The pizza, that'll be plain cheese.

www.ingramcontent.com/pod-product-compliance
Ingram Content Group UK Ltd.
Pitfield, Milton Keynes, MK11 3LW, UK
UKHW022224230426
12048UKWH00016BA/1042